THE SUR

Sharon Derwent, a nurse on the children's ward of the South City General, is stunned when the eminent heart surgeon Bryce Townshend asks her to marry him. What chance does such a marriage stand of surviving the stresses and strains of working together in the big Melbourne hospital particularly when neither partner is in love?

THE SURGEON'S WIFE

BY
JUDITH WORTHY

MILLS & BOON LIMITED
London · Sydney · Toronto

First published in Great Britain 1983
by Mills & Boon Limited, 15–16 Brook's Mews,
London W1A 1DR

© Judith Worthy 1983

Australian copyright 1983
Philippine copyright 1983

ISBN 0 263 74177 X

All the characters in this book have no existence outside
the imagination of the Author, and have no relation
whatsoever to anyone bearing the same name or names.
They are not even distantly inspired by any individual
known or unknown to the Author, and all the incidents
are pure invention.

The text of this publication or any part thereof may not be
reproduced or transmitted in any form or by any means,
electronic or mechanical, including photocopying,
recording, storage in an information retrieval system,
or otherwise, without the written permission of the
publisher.

This book is sold subject to the condition that it shall not,
by way of trade or otherwise, be lent, resold, hired out or
otherwise circulated without the prior consent of the
publisher in any form of binding or cover other than that
in which it is published and without a similar condition
including this condition being imposed on the subsequent
purchaser.

03/0183

Set in 10 on 10½ pt Linotron Times

Photoset by Rowland Phototypesetting Ltd
Bury St Edmunds, Suffolk
Made and printed in Great Britain by
Richard Clay (The Chaucer Press) Ltd
Bungay, Suffolk

CHAPTER ONE

'Mm . . . mmm . . . I like it!' Janna exclaimed appreciatively, as Sharon twirled in front of her in the new dark green silk dress she had bought only that day. 'You ought to put your hair up though.' She eyed Sharon critically, and grinned. 'That is, if you really want to wow the guy!'

Sharon Derwent felt a rush of colour to her cheeks. She stepped back to take a long appraising look at herself in the mirror. At Janna's insistence she held up her thick auburn hair to test the effect of a swept-up style with the new dress.

'It would take a few minutes,' she said doubtfully. 'Have I got time?'

'He'll wait for you,' said Janna positively. 'Go on, do it. It's about time someone saw you for the warm-blooded voluptuous creature that you really are!' She perched on Sharon's bed, drew her knees up and hugged them. 'And Townshend needs someone to thaw him out.'

Sharon turned to look at her as she smoothed her thick lustrous hair into a french roll, and pinned it securely. The shorter hair at the front waved attractively across her forehead and the whole effect was to emphasise her slender neck and oval face. Her well-defined eyebrows suddenly dipped towards each other above her green-flecked brown eyes, and there was a puzzled look in them, as well as a quizzical twist to her slightly parted lips as she said:

'I really don't know why he asked me . . .'

'Because he fancies you, why else?' rejoined Janna, rocking back and forth on the bed. She grinned teasingly. 'You'd better watch out. Beneath that carefully starched clinical white coat there no doubt beats a heart of violent passion.'

'I hardly think so,' said Sharon. 'He's always very aloof . . .'

'And infuriatingly arrogant,' added Janna candidly. 'I've always had the feeling that he regards everyone below the rank of consultant as barely worth his attention. He's always rubbing somebody up the wrong way.'

'It's just his manner,' Sharon said defensively, feeling that perhaps they were doing the man an injustice. 'He's very popular with the patients—at least he is with the children. I don't know about in the other wards.'

Janna said reflectively, 'He *is* attractive . . . in an enigmatic sort of way . . . and I've heard one or two say he's got sexy eyes. Do you think he's sexy, Sharon?'

'I've never thought about it,' said Sharon, clipping on a pair of small gold earrings, and knew it was a lie.

She was not willing to admit to Janna what she grudgingly admitted to herself—that Dr Bryce Townshend, Senior Cardiac Surgeon at South City General, the big Melbourne hospital where she was a staff nurse, and her flatmate, Janna Wills, a secretary, did have rivetting dark grey eyes that made her shiver with an odd sort of pleasure sometimes when he looked at her, despite his apparent indifference to her.

He had dark wavy hair, a broad high forehead, and a rather surprisingly sensual mouth under a straight, uncompromising nose, but she had never thought of him as sexy. There was a certain fascination about him, that was all, because he was so aloof. He rarely spoke except in monosyllables, unless he was angry, and he was so dedicated to his work in the Cardiology Unit that his colleagues joked that he was aiming for a Nobel Prize.

If he sometimes seemed arrogant, then he probably had reason to be. He was a perfectionist, a man who did not suffer fools gladly, and incompetence sent him into a rage, as many a sister and staff nurse had discovered to her cost. Sharon had clashed with him on more than one occasion, and afterwards she'd had to admit that there had been some justification for his annoyance.

Whether the redoubtable Dr Townshend had any personal life, and whether there was anyone special in it, had long been the subject of speculation around the hospital, but Dr Townshend was totally unforthcoming, even to his closest colleagues.

In the year she had been at South City General Hospital, Sharon had encountered him quite regularly since she nursed many of his patients in her ward, which was Children's Surgical—but nicknamed Pinocchio. Mostly he had been polite, but always as stand-offish with her as he was with everyone else. She had never had any reason to believe he regarded her any differently from any of the other nurses. He was always quick to criticize if something was not as he expected it to be, and certainly had shown no preference for her. Their occasional brief conversations were mostly about the patients.

That he had a softer side, Sharon was often aware. She would watch him sometimes and marvel at the change in him when he was with the children. His face would light up for a child the way it never did for anyone else. And children obviously adored him. She had noticed too that if a child died, he would be more withdrawn than ever for a time, his darkly handsome features would become quite gaunt, and she always had the feeling that he blamed himself. With children he was natural and outgoing, with adults he was withdrawn as though afraid to reveal the real Bryce Townshend.

And then one day a couple of months ago he had astonished Sharon by deliberately seeking her out after she had thought he had left the ward. She was filing away treatment notes when he came into the duty room, perched casually on the edge of the desk, and engaged her in conversation. On first seeing him she had tensed herself to receive some rebuke or criticism, and was conscious of Sister Garland watching curiously from her office, through the glass panel separating them.

But Dr Townshend had not come to show displeasure. He talked first about one of the children who was to have a hole-in-the-heart operation, and Sharon thought that was all he wanted to talk to her about. Somehow the conversation veered to other subjects, and in the course of it they discovered a mutual love of classical music, and a particular preference for Beethoven.

Looking steadily at her, he had said casually. 'I often go to concerts at the Town Hall. Might see you there some time.'

Taken aback, she had answered, 'Yes . . . I suppose so . . .' She had thought little more about it except to decide privately that when he did thaw a little the dedicated heart surgeon could be quite charming. She had, however, attached no real significance to the conversation.

So, it had come as a complete surprise when yesterday he had again lingered after his round of the ward, waiting until Sister was out of the way before he came quickly to the point.

'I've got a couple of tickets to a Beethoven concert tomorrow night. I was wondering if . . . if you're not already going . . . if you'd like to come with me.'

Sharon had almost dropped the sheaf of reports she was holding, and had stood staring at him dumbfounded for a long moment, probably, she thought ruefully afterwards, with her mouth hanging open like an awed first-year student nurse.

He had said diffidently, 'I know it's short notice. You've probably got something else to do.'

Sharon found her voice at last. 'I . . . er . . . no, as a matter of fact I haven't. I'd love to come.'

'Good. I'll pick you up about seven.' He had smiled at her, but his tone was still as brusque as usual.

Before Sharon could say another word he had gone, and she had been left staring at the space where he had stood, wondering if she was subject to hallucinations all at once. Thinking about it later she realised that he had not asked where she lived, or even if she would be off duty. He had evidently found out those facts for himself. Dr Townshend was nothing if not thorough. She had finished her shift in a daze, unable to explain the sudden change in his attitude.

His invitation, she reflected now as she put the finishing touches to her make-up, was certainly not as Janna had suggested, because he fancied her, but simply because he happened to have found out quite by accident that she liked Beethoven. It was more than likely that his usual concert companion had let him down.

Now, when she said as much to Janna, her flatmate was scornful. 'I don't believe he's got a girl-friend. He asked you because he wanted to.' She slid off Sharon's bed. 'I must dash and have my shower. Peter'll be here any minute.'

She breezed out of Sharon's room, singing lustily one of the newest rock numbers, while Sharon smiled to herself. For once Janna was bound to be wrong. Her greeny-brown eyes looking back at her from the mirror reflected her nervousness, but underlying it there was a warm tingling sensation of anticipation. What would it be like, dating Dr Townshend?

When the doorbell rang, Sharon's heart quickened its beat, and as Janna was still in the shower, she went to answer it. It was Janna's boyfriend, Peter.

'Come in, Peter,' Sharon said, but felt just a small twinge of apprehension. *He* was late. What if he didn't turn up at all?

'Say . . . that's a classy bit of gear,' Peter remarked, with a low whistle and a mockingly lascivious look as he sidled around Sharon, looking her up and down.

Sharon laughed. Peter sprawled on the couch and continued to eye her admiringly. 'Big date?'

Sharon shrugged. 'I'm going to a concert at the Town Hall.'

Peter's mouth turned down. 'Better you than me. Must be some guy, huh?' He smoothed his dark hair and added laughingly, 'Sure you wouldn't rather come to the disco with Janna and me?'

'Not tonight,' said Sharon. She did occasionally go with them, and she enjoyed disco music and dancing, but she always felt a little uncomfortable as she was four years older than Janna. At twenty-five you were practically a wrinkly in some people's eyes.

Janna sailed in, resplendent in a dark blue satin cat-suit, her blonde hair flowing in soft waves over her shoulders, her pretty vivacious features expertly made up. Peter's eyes devoured her proprietorially, and Sharon smiled to herself. She expected Janna and Peter to become engaged at any time.

Rather to her surprise Janna, who seemed such a worldly young woman, even though younger than herself, had categorically stated that she had no intention of entering into a trial marriage. It was all or nothing for her, she had declared emphatically when they had once discussed it. Sharon had agreed. If you loved someone, she thought, you would want to marry them. She knew that if she was not sure, then she would not want to live with that person until she was.

'Ready, Jan?' Peter swung his long legs off the couch and leapt up.

Janna turned to Sharon with a cheeky grin. 'I hope you get your money's worth out of old Beethoven . . . and Dr Townshend!' As she spoke the doorbell rang again. Her eyebrows flew up, and she said in a hoarse whisper, 'That'll be him now!'

Sharon tensed inside. She let Janna rush to open the door since her friend was so eager to do so.

'Hello, Dr Townshend,' Janna was greeting him in a very deferential voice. 'Please come in.'

She ushered him into the living room, and Sharon was immediately struck by how tall and broad-shouldered he looked against the diminutive Janna, and how different he seemed out of his white doctor's coat. He was wearing dark grey trousers, and a deep maroon velvet jacket

over a pale grey shirt and maroon tie. His eyes met hers
for a moment, then slid slowly down over her in a look
that was quite uncharacteristic of the Dr Townshend she
was used to. For a moment she could not utter a word.

It did not matter. Janna was not so afflicted, and
rushed on breathlessly, 'Peter and I are just going. Come
on, Peter.' She grabbed his arm and almost pushed him
out of the door. 'Have a good time and don't do anything
we wouldn't enjoy!' she called roguishly over her shoulder.

The front door slammed and they were gone, leaving
the echoes of their 'good nights' reverberating around
the room. Sharon was now alone with Dr Townshend
and more nervous than she had thought possible.

He treated her to a rather anxious look. 'I hope we
won't be the subject of hospital gossip tomorrow.'

Sharon drew a sharp breath. 'Of course not! Janna is
very discreet, and so, as a matter of fact, am I!' She could
not help the slight indignation that coloured her tone.
She suspected that he was regretting already the impulse
that had made him ask her out.

He moved closer. 'I'm sorry . . . I didn't mean . . .'
He looked disconcerted now. 'But you know what hospitals are!'

'I do indeed,' she answered coolly, 'and for a senior
surgeon to invite a staff nurse to accompany him to a
concert would certainly be cause for gossip. It was really
very kind of you to invite me, Dr Townshend . . .'

He was looking down at her with a quizzical expression in his eyes. 'My name is Bryce.' His deep,
measured tones seemed to convey more than his
words. 'It was kind of you, Sharon, to say yes.'

They continued to look at each other for a long, rather
uncomfortable moment, during which Sharon was pos-
sessed of conflicting and rather startling desires—either
to run away, or to rush into his arms. It was the second
alternative that was the most shatteringly unexpected,
and she had the ghastly feeling that he knew exactly what

her reactions were and was secretly amused.

He glanced at his watch. 'We still have time to stop somewhere for a drink on the way.'

Sharon began to recover her wits. 'I'll just get my bag . . .' She crossed the room to where she had left her black silk clutch purse on the sideboard, and as she did so a thought struck her. She turned to him. 'We could have a drink here if you like. Janna and I don't drink much but we do keep sherry and whisky, and I—think there might be some brandy left from Christmas.'

He chuckled. 'For medicinal purposes only, of course!' His laughter was warm and vibrant. Sharon had seldom heard him laugh, except with the children in the ward, and it sounded strange—as though he was a different person from the Dr Townshend she knew. He was saying, 'A whisky would be fine . . . unless you'd rather go somewhere else?'

Sharon was content to stay in the flat and said so. She hoped she would be able to dispel some of the awkwardness of the situation by staying a little longer on home ground, rather than going to some smart cocktail bar.

'Please sit down . . .' she invited.

She fetched two glasses from the kitchen cupboard and poured out a whisky for Bryce, placing it on the table near him together with a small jug of water. He smiled. 'Thanks.'

Sharon poured herself a small dry sherry and as he was sitting on the couch she perched on the arm of one of the chairs.

He glanced around. 'Pleasant little flat you've got. Have you and Janna been sharing long?'

'About a year. It's actually Janna's flat.'

He chuckled. 'I can see that!'

Sharon was surprised at his perception. The bright decor and modern furnishings which were typical of Janna could also be her taste, for all he knew. He knew nothing about her. As it happened her tastes were more subdued, and were given free rein in her own room, which of course he could not see.

'You're not much alike, are you?' His question seemed to imply that he found the fact of their sharing a flat rather puzzling.

'Not really,' Sharon admitted, 'but we get along very well. Janna is wonderfully good-natured. She knew I was looking for a flat so when her flatmate went overseas she asked me if I'd like to take her place. It's close to the hospital and suits me very well.'

There was a mocking glint in his eyes. 'Close enough for riding your bike to work!'

Sharon blushed. The fact that he had noticed her made her feel unnecessarily embarrassed. 'Well . . . yes, I do ride my bike to the hospital . . .'

'And very elegantly you do so,' he said, and his eyes were half teasing, but half something else too enigmatic for her to identify.

Teasing was not quite what she had expected from Dr Townshend but it did make him seem a little more human. It surprised her that he had even noticed her riding her bicycle. Her mode of transport caused some amusement amongst her colleagues and friends but she was accustomed to their ribbing. She had always ridden a bike everywhere at home which was in the country, and it was a quick and convenient way to get to and from the hospital, a good way to avoid traffic jams and delays on public transport. She'd owned an elderly Mini a couple of years ago but her brother, at university then, had borrowed it and smashed it up, thankfully with only minor damage to himself. Sharon had decided not to replace it, at least for the time being.

'I find it a cheap and convenient way to commute,' she said, taking a sip of sherry.

Bryce surprised her again. 'It's good exercise too. More cyclists and we might have less coronaries cluttering up our wards. I ride a bike myself quite a lot.'

'Do you really!' She was astonished. It did not fit her image of him at all. She could not imagine the aloof Dr

Townshend letting his hair down and belting along on a bike. Inwardly she rebuked herself. He was human, after all. It was just that the remoteness she was accustomed to seemed to overshadow any other side to him.

He nodded, then drained his glass and glanced at his watch again. 'I think we'd better make tracks. I hate arriving late. It's scarcely polite to the orchestra.' He stood up, and Sharon did too. He looked her over again, his dark, slightly narrowed eyes, shaded by dark bushy brows, rather intense, but there was an unexpectedly whimsical tilt to his wide, firm mouth as though he found her rather diverting. He said casually, 'Will you need a wrap?'

Sharon smiled at the old-fashioned word. 'I don't think so. It's a very warm night.'

He touched her arm briefly. 'Shall we go then?'

Sharon picked up her clutch bag, closed the flat door and followed him down the stairs. She did not feel any more at ease with him now than she had at the beginning, in spite of his having put their relationship on a more informal basis by asking her to call him Bryce. It still seemed a little impertinent to do so. He was still Dr Townshend, and very much her superior. It was hard to think of herself on equal terms with him, even on a social occasion away from the hospital. The shadow of South City General stood between them with all its strict discipline and protocol, which traditionally persisted despite a more modern and democratic administration. Sharon was sure Bryce felt it too and regretted his rashness in asking her to go to the concert.

His elegant grey Mercedes was parked conspicuously in the street just outside the block of flats. It was not quite dark yet, but the street lights were beginning to flicker on. Bryce opened the passenger door for Sharon and she slid into the seat somewhat awkwardly because she was nervous, and because she was not accustomed to such a luxurious mode of travel. He bent and lifted the skirt of her dress so that it should not be caught in the car door when he slammed it, and when he tucked the folds of the full skirt inside the car his hand brushed against her thigh briefly, sending an unexpected tremor through her.

She ought to have known it would be like this, she thought ruefully, as they joined the stream of traffic heading towards the city. She ought to have known she would feel awkward, out of place, and thoroughly uneasy in his company. She should have refused the invitation. Why on earth had he asked her? He ought to have known it would be an uncomfortable evening for them both.

The floodlit bulk of the Shrine of Remembrance slid past and the glittering towers of the city loomed up ahead, stark and bold against the darkening sky. Sharon glanced down at the reflections in the Yarra as they stopped briefly behind a tram on Princes Bridge, and wished the evening was over.

Bryce had been silent since they left the flat, and she had been unable to think of anything to say, even concerning the hospital. She was so afraid of sounding gauche or trivial. They might both like Beethoven, but that was all they would have in common, she was sure. Bryce Townshend's world was vastly different from hers.

'We're still in good time,' he remarked as they left the car and walked the short distance to the Town Hall. People were steadily flowing in, and Sharon began to feel a little better once she became part of the crowd. Her anticipation of the music also helped to dull the uneasiness she felt with Bryce. He bought a programme which he handed to her, and then gallantly kept a guiding hand at her elbow as they entered the auditorium and were shown their seats.

Their seats were excellent ones, with a good view of the whole orchestra. He must have had them for some time, Sharon thought. This seemed to confirm that his regular companion had let him down at the last minute. For the few minutes left before the programme started they exchanged a few inconsequential remarks and comments about the music they were to hear. The final offering was to be the Seventh Symphony, and Sharon was pleased to be able to mention that quite recently she had bought a new recording of this particular symphony. Bryce was interested and asked her about it.

'Perhaps you'll let me hear it sometime,' he remarked in a smiling aside.

Surprised, she said at once, 'Yes, of course. I'll bring the record in for you.'

There was a flicker of something in his eyes that was half quizzical, half something else, and Sharon had the oddest feeling that she had offended him in some way, although she could not think for the life of her how.

When the concert began Sharon soon realised that she was not going to be able to give all her attention to the music as she usually did. Part of her was acutely conscious of the man who sat beside her, his large frame filling the seat, and making her feel quite small, although at five foot five she was not as petite as Janna. Several times she had the distinct impression that his gaze had shifted from looking straight ahead at the orchestra to contemplating her, and once, to prove herself fanciful, she turned her head slightly. To her dismay, he was looking at her, and she caught his eye. He just smiled enigmatically and swept his gaze back to the front, leaving Sharon feeling that she had been caught out looking at him.

'Well, did you enjoy it?' Bryce asked as they were leaving the hall at the end of the concert. 'You applauded as though you had.'

Sharon went pink. Had she embarrassed him by clapping too loudly? 'Yes, I did, very much, thank you,' she said, aware that she was being a little dishonest. She had enjoyed the music, but she was not sure she had enjoyed being with him. She admired him as a surgeon, and he commanded her deepest respect professionally, but separating the surgeon from the man seemed an insuperable task. Her attitudes were too deeply ingrained. She could not feel at ease with him, and she knew suddenly that having gone out with him tonight would make their encounters at the hospital less rather than more comfortable.

As the crowd spilled onto the footpath, Sharon felt Bryce's hand firmly attach itself to her elbow. Momentarily, as a large group of people surged past them, she was crushed against him. His arm slid protectively around her and drew her towards the edge of the footpath.

He smiled down into her face. 'I'd like some coffee, wouldn't you?'

Sharon nodded. 'If you like.' She ought to have said she would rather go straight home, she realised, but it was too late now.

Again, as he released her, his look was quizzical, and faintly offended. 'There's a nice little place in a lane just off Little Collins Street.'

Sharon let him steer her through the groups of concert-goers standing chatting in the warm still night, up the narrow dark street, and down some steps to the coffee bar. A loud hubbub rose to greet them even before Bryce pushed open the door. The place was smoke-filled and very crowded. His face showed his distaste.

'Everybody's got here before us,' he said, adding, 'Is there anywhere else close by?'

'There's Angelo's,' Sharon said. 'That's not far.'

He seemed to know it. 'Ah . . . yes . . .' He cupped her elbow in his large hand, taking a firm grip this time and they retraced their steps, walking the short distance to the coffee bar she had named. The same situation met them there, only it was worse because several people were queuing in the entrance.

Bryce frowned and shook his head. 'Queuing for coffee is not my idea of a pleasant end to an evening.'

'It doesn't matter,' said Sharon, feeling sure he was

only trying to please her. Coffee bars were probably not
the sort of places he frequented.

'I suppose we could try the Southern Cross,' he suggested, naming a large hotel. His eyes rested speculatively on her. 'On the other hand, it would be almost as
quick to go to my place . . .' A faint smile hovered on his
lips so that Sharon again had the feeling that he was
amused by her, '. . . that is if you don't object.'

She could hardly say she did, so she asked, 'Where do
you live?'

'Just the other side of Fitzroy Gardens,' he answered,
and with a self-mocking smile. 'I'm an East Melbourne
fan. I like the old style architecture, the air of decayed
grandeur that pervades the place.'

They were not far from where he had parked the car,
and were soon at the top end of the city, and turning into
one of the small side streets. Sharon, too, was fond of
this part of old Melbourne, with its once stately man-
sions, gracious two and three-storeyed terraces and
villas, many with iron lace decorated balconies and
verandahs, intricate paving, fancy rendering and pat-
terned brickwork. Many of the old houses had been
restored and with its tranquil tree-shaded streets, this
part of Melbourne retained a quiet elegance and was a
small oasis amid the hurly-burly of the city.

The car purred smoothly to a halt under a street light
outside a Victorian villa of two stories. The ubiquitous
iron lace scalloped the verandah and the balcony above,
a weeping birch filled the garden on one side of the
central pathway, and a jacaranda umbrellaed the rest of
the narrow space. They entered through a wrought-iron
gate in the high bluestone wall, and were greeted by
stone lions on plinths flanking the stone steps up to the
front door. Carriage lamps on either side of the door cast
a welcoming light.

'I wish I could afford a flat in a house like this!' Sharon
exclaimed spontaneously. Suddenly, the flat where she
and Janna lived seemed very drab and grimly functional.

'Actually I own the house,' Bryce answered briefly, as he turned the key in the door.

Sharon felt she had been naïve, and had made a bit of a gaffe. She ought to have known that a man in his position might own the whole house. To cover her embarrassment, she said lightly, 'It's a big house for just one person.'

The door was open and Bryce stood aside to let Sharon go in ahead of him. He had switched on a light in the hall, and their eyes met briefly. He said quite casually, 'Yes, it is. I bought it quite a few years ago when . . . when I was living with someone.'

Sharon wished she had not spoken. She was taken aback by his admission but did her best not to show it. She made no comment, but simply let the remark pass, leaving him to elaborate if he wished. She did not want him to think she was curious. She was more than that, she realised at once. She was a little disappointed.

'Come into the drawing room,' he invited, pushing open one of a pair of glass doors on their left.

The elegance of the hall was repeated in the drawing room which was a large high-ceilinged room with a massive fireplace, ornate ceiling mouldings, and narrow floor-to-ceiling sash windows curtained in brown velvet. The tones of the decor were warm browns and creams with touches of orange. There was a decidedly masculine air about it, Sharon decided, looking at the antique furniture, the plain but comfortable loose-covered sofas, the softly shaded lamps, as Bryce flicked on switches and then doused the central light. Although the furnishings were obviously expensive, there was nothing ostentatious about the room. Sharon was immediately interested in the many pictures that were displayed to advantage on plain off-white walls. Even her inexperienced eye could see that they were mostly originals, and that there were several very familiar and famous styles among them.

Bryce saw the direction of her gaze. 'My father was an

amateur art collector,' he told her, with a warmth of tone
that made her glance quickly at him. He must have been
fond of his father, she thought. He went on, 'He bought
paintings from his friends, and friends of friends. More
by accident than design he acquired works by Australian
artists who are now very well known.' He did not,
however, offer any further information about his family.

'This is a beautiful room,' Sharon said in a slightly
hushed voice. But she felt out of place in it. She did not
belong in this kind of atmosphere. It underlined the vast
gulf between her and Dr Townshend. She wished she
hadn't come. She was not his kind of person at all, she
thought regretfully, reluctantly acknowledging that she
would like to be.

'Make yourself at home, Sharon,' Bryce said, 'and I'll
put the coffee on.' He pushed open another set of double
doors which Sharon saw led to an equally elegant dining
room, and presumably thence to the kitchen.

'Can I do anything?' she offered.

He turned to smile at her, the slow enigmatic smile he
had treated her to several times tonight. He said in a low
tone, 'No. Amuse yourself looking at the pictures. I
shan't be long. My housekeeper, Betsy, always leaves
supper for me. She has a small flat at the rear of the
house and she is what they used to call in bygone days a
"treasure". I inherited her along with everything else
from my parents.'

While he was gone, Sharon toured the room slowly,
savouring it. She stroked satin-smooth wood, traced
with a finger the patterns on tapestry-covered chairs,
and paused to admire a set of ebony chessmen set out on
an inlaid board. She burned with curiosity about the
woman he had lived with but knew she would never dare
ask about her.

When Bryce returned carrying a silver tray set with
cups and saucers, a coffee pot and a plate of biscuits,
Sharon was staring into a glass-fronted cabinet full of
oriental curios. She did not realise he had returned until

he came and stood beside her, making her jump.

'Sorry . . .' He reached out and opened the cabinet doors, brushing her arm with his as he did so. He turned to look inquiringly at her. 'You're interested in oriental art?'

Sharon took an involuntary step back. 'I don't know anything about art, but Asia has always fascinated me more than Europe. It's so mysterious!' She waited for him to laugh but he did not, so she went on, 'I went to Singapore for a holiday once, and I always go to Indonesian and Chinese exhibitions and that sort of thing. And I love Little Bourke Street!'

He would be bound to laugh at her now, she knew, but he didn't. He merely looked at her with interest. 'It's a wonder we haven't run into each other there. I confess to a passion for Chinese restaurants.'

'Janna and I go to a very good place . . .' Sharon began enthusiastically, then stopped. He would be interested in more sophisticated places than the cheap café which she and her flatmate patronised. She peered into the cabinet again. 'Did your father collect all this too?'

'No!' He laughed self-deprecatingly. 'These are my little weakness. I worked in hospitals in Malaya, Thailand and also Vietnam after I qualified. I used to spend my spare time picking up odds and ends. Not with any knowledge of their value, I hasten to add. I bought what I loved the look of or the feel of. I never had any intention of trying to profit from the hobby.'

He showed her several carved jade ornaments that Sharon was sure were bound to be valuable, and when he handed her a delicate porcelain figurine, she held it for a moment and then gave it back.

'I'm scared I might drop it!'

He replaced it in the cabinet saying, 'You can have a good look another time. Come on, or the coffee will be cold.'

They crossed the room to where he had placed the tray on a low coffee table in front of one of the sofas. 'If you

wouldn't mind pouring, Sharon, I'll put some music on,'
he said. 'A Beethoven sonata would be soothing, don't
you think, for this time of night?'

Sharon murmured her agreement and poured the
coffee, thinking all the time of what he had said. 'You
can have a good look another time.' Did that mean he
intended to bring her here again, or had it just been a slip
of the tongue?

Bryce sat near her on the couch, leaning back com-
fortably, one foot resting across his other knee as he
drank his coffee. Sharon perched a little more formally
on the edge of the cushions, leaning against the arm at
one end.

After a brief silence, he suddenly said, 'You're the
best nurse we've had on Children's Surgical, you know,
Sharon.'

Deep colour flooded her cheeks, already warmed by
the coffee. 'I'm sure that's not true,' she muttered,
flustered by the unexpected compliment.

'You're a natural,' he said, then added casually, 'I
suppose you'll be leaving us to get married and have kids
of your own before long.'

Sharon was startled at such a personal question. 'I . . .
I hadn't thought about it.' She managed a light laugh.
'I'll have to find a husband first!' Then she wished she
had not said that in case it seemed pointed.

He merely said, 'No steady boyfriend?'

'No.' Since she had broken off a fairly long-standing
relationship with a radiologist at the hospital where she
had worked before going to South City General, Sharon
had shied away from involvements. She was never short
of dates but she seldom went out with one man more
than a few times, and always made it clear that she
valued her freedom and intended to keep it for the time
being. But there was no need, surely, to elaborate to Dr
Townshend.

He chuckled. 'I suppose a hospital is as good a place
for husband . . . or wife-hunting as anywhere.'

Sharon did not answer, and he was silent for a moment or two. They finished their coffee, and Sharon refused a second cup. Bryce did not press her. The record clicked off and he rose.

'I suppose I'd better let you get your beauty sleep. I've got a heavy day tomorrow myself.'

Sharon suddenly remembered. 'You're operating on Jamie Wilson in the morning, aren't you?'

He nodded gravely.

'It's not a good prognosis, is it?' Sharon said slowly.

'No.' His eyes were in shadow and she could not see his expression but the rest of his face was suddenly tense, and she felt a pang of anxiety for him.

On him depended the life of a child of five with a complicated congenital heart condition that had already necessitated several operations. She knew that tomorrow's would probably be the last. If it failed, Jamie could, at best, look forward to the life of an invalid, or at worst have a year or less to live. For the first time she felt what it must be like to be the surgeon in whose hands the fragile thread of life so often lay, on whose expertise the strengthening or snapping of that thread depended. If the child died it would not be Bryce's fault, and yet she knew he would blame himself.

'Come along . . . I'll take you home,' he said, in the brusque tone she knew so well. Almost as though he was bored with her suddenly and wanted to get rid of her.

Sharon picked up her bag from the arm of the couch and followed him out to the car. The traffic was negligible now and they reached her block of flats within a few minutes. The drive was completed in almost total silence. Sharon suspected that his thoughts were all for the operations he had to perform tomorrow. No, today, she thought, realising it was well after midnight. Was that why he had invited her to the concert tonight, to take his mind off it for a few hours? But he faced serious and difficult operations almost every day. Surely it couldn't have been just that.

'There's no need for you to come up with me,' Sharon said, as he escorted her to the entrance to the block.

'I'll see you right to your door,' he insisted.

Sharon pressed the time-switch inside the entrance, the light came on, and they mounted to the second floor. Outside the flat door Sharon fumbled for her key, saying to Bryce as she did so, 'Thank you very much for the concert. I really did enjoy it very much . . . and thank you for the coffee . . .'

'I enjoyed it very much too,' he said formally. 'We must do it again some time.'

It was not so much a slip of the tongue now, Sharon thought, as just polite but meaningless words. She was sure he did not intend to ask her out again.

'Well, thanks again,' she murmured. 'I hope Jamie's operation will be a success. I shan't be in until the afternoon. Good night . . .'

He made no move to go and his penetrating gaze was beginning to unnerve her. When the time-switch suddenly clicked off and Sharon reached out in the darkness to press it in again, she found her wrist caught in a strong grip and prevented from reaching it.

Then his arms were around her, holding her tightly against him, as his lips found hers unerringly in the dark. He kissed her with a precision that reminded her that he was a mature and experienced man. He had caught her off guard, and deprived of the power to rationalise, she found herself responding to him with rather more readiness than she might have done otherwise. There was something about being in almost total darkness that made her forget for a moment who he was.

How long that kiss might have lasted, Sharon would never know, because suddenly the light snapped on again, and she heard the street door closing, and voices drifting up the stairs. Janna and Peter. Bryce released her and they looked at each other for a moment, dazzled by the light. Then Sharon saw what she believed was a mocking smile on his lips, and she felt angry.

'There was no need to do that!' she accused reproach-
fully.

His eyebrows rose fractionally. 'Isn't that how an
evening like this is supposed to end?'

'No,' she answered flatly, stung by the inference that
she had expected him to kiss her. 'Good night, Dr
Townshend.'

'Good night, Sharon.' He swiftly tilted her chin and
lightly brushed his lips against hers. 'Don't be too angry
with me.'

He was turning to go just as Janna and Peter burst
breathlessly onto the landing.

'Oops, sorry!' exclaimed Janna, with a wide-eyed
glance from Bryce to Sharon. Then, more soberly she
said, 'Hello, Dr Townshend. How was the concert?'

'Very enjoyable,' he answered. 'I hope you had a
good time too.'

'Yes, it was great,' said Janna.

Bryce wished them a brisk good night and Sharon
heard him descending the stairs at least two at a time,
as though he couldn't escape quickly enough.

'Hey . . . did we gatecrash your big scene?' demanded
Janna as they all went into the flat. 'He looked about as
happy as a hiatus hernia. I know! He made a pass at you
and you walloped him one!'

Sharon said stonily, 'He just brought me home . . .'

'And you just happen to like saying goodnight in the
dark,' said Janna wickedly.

'The light had just gone out and I was about to push it
on when you did.' Sharon knew she wasn't being very
convincing.

'So that's how your lipstick got smudged,' said Janna
mockingly. She giggled. 'All right . . . no teasing! What
about some coffee everybody?'

'Not for me thanks,' said Sharon. 'I've already had
some.'

She said goodnight and retreated quickly to her room,
disgusted to find that she was trembling all over.

CHAPTER TWO

JANNA had already left in the morning when Sharon finally surfaced, feeling rather more jaded than the previous evening's outing warranted. Her head ached a little, and she felt unaccountably depressed. She was glad she did not have to face her flatmate's ribald comments, or her close questioning about the concert and Dr Townshend. Janna would probe for details later, without doubt, but by then Sharon hoped to be in a better frame of mind to deal with her friend's curiosity.

She moved slowly about the compact little kitchen, making coffee and toast, and while waiting for the one to pop up, the other to filter, she gazed idly out of the window across the treetops in nearby suburban gardens towards the city. In the middle distance she could see the solid red-brick outline of South City General, and beyond the last century facade of the old building the more clinical lines of the recent cream brick extensions.

Breakfast would be over in the wards by now. Doctors would be doing their rounds soon, with sisters in attendance, while hundreds of nurses like herself would be flying about doing the thousand and one tasks needed to keep the busy hospital running smoothly. And Bryce Townshend—perhaps at this very moment he was scrubbing up, ready to operate on tiny, fragile Jamie Wilson with the spiky fair hair and enormous blue eyes that gave him the appealing look of a mischievous waif, and had caused even dour Sister Garland to remark: 'That young man's going to break a few hearts before he's finished!'

Sharon had thought sadly, 'If his own survives the ordeal of yet another operation.'

She swallowed hard on the lump that had suddenly

come into her throat, and automatically her index and middle fingers on both hands crossed and were clenched tight.

'Don't let him die,' she whispered, and then quickly turned her head away from the bright blue morning outside the window.

From the main roads converging on the city came the muted rumble of trams, the hum of cars, interspersed with the rattle of trains. People in their thousands were rushing to work, some of them passing right under the somewhat forbidding red-brick walls of South City General, few of them giving a thought to the high drama daily being played out within—none of them aware that a small boy's life hung in the balance this morning.

The coffee finished filtering with its usual rather rude-sounding slurp, and at the same moment the toast popped up. Sharon sat down to her solitary breakfast, still sunk in the lethargy which had been with her since she had woken.

Inevitably her thoughts returned to the previous night, but she was unable to analyse her feelings accurately. Looking back it seemed that despite her nervousness she had in fact enjoyed the evening, although the moment when Bryce had kissed her had left her with a feeling she could not quite come to terms with. A sudden rush of warm blood through her veins reminded her how she had felt when his lips touched hers, demanding a response from her in a way that could not be denied.

She felt angry with herself for reacting so brazenly, at the same time astonished that he should have been able to arouse such a surge of feeling in her. She also felt embarrassed, remembering what he had said afterwards. He had thought it was what she expected. How was she going to look him in the eye again? Never had she experienced such a conflict of emotions as she did this morning. No man before had left her feeling so confused.

'It's only because he's Dr Townshend,' she said aloud

in a firm voice as she lathered vigorously under the shower.

She was making too much of it. He was not likely to ask her out again. The best thing to do was to forget the whole thing. But that was what she could not do straight away. All morning, as she shopped for necessities for her and Janna's meals, did some washing and leisurely Hoovered the flat, she kept catching herself thinking about Bryce Townshend again and again. Why had he asked her to go to the concert last night? None of the solutions she had so far considered really seemed to fit, and the mystery remained.

That afternoon when she wheeled her bicycle out of the lock-up storeroom which she and Janna used, behind the block of flats, and set off for the hospital, her thoughts were on a different track. She could hardly wait to get there and learn the outcome of Jamie Wilson's operation. Several times during the day she had been tempted to ring and ask about him, but each time she had resisted it, forestalled by the irrational superstition that she would hear what she did not want to hear.

In any case the Gargoyle was on this morning and she would have thought her sentimental. Nurses should not become involved with or attached to their patients was her credo, because, Sister Garland maintained, it affected their work. Sharon agreed in principle, but where children were concerned she felt that what they needed most when in hospital was love. She could not, in any case, help becoming involved, especially with children like Jamie Wilson who were more courageous than many adults she had nursed.

Sharon pedalled expertly through the traffic, ignoring occasional wolf-whistles from passing cars, a minor hazard to which she was accustomed. Within a few minutes she was turning into the hospital yard, past the ambulance bays and the doctors' car park, noticing as she did so that Bryce Townshend's grey Mercedes was still there. Her heart gave an annoying lurch as she experienced a mixture of pleasure and apprehension, both of which were foolish since she would not necessarily see him today.

When the lift doors opened and Sharon stepped into the lift that would take her up to her ward on the third floor, she was so preoccupied that she did not notice the other passenger. Consequently she walked right into the arms of Norton Fitzgerald, one of the junior doctors.

'Lovely, lovely Rose of Sharon . . .' he murmured, clasping her firmly to his chest as the doors closed behind her.

Sharon struggled in vain. 'Norton . . . please . . .' She was unable to extricate herself, and even violently shaking her head was no deterrent to the determined Dr Fitzgerald, the hospital flirt.

'Doesn't know the meaning of the word "no",' someone had said once, receiving the droll reply, 'He thinks it's yes!'

Everyone liked Norton, however, and quite a few nurses had crushes on him. He was tall, with light brown curly hair and a handsome little-boy's face, in which brilliant blue eyes sparkled with charm. When he smiled at them, his women patients wondered how they could wangle an extra few days under his care and even the toughest sister was putty in his hands. He had littered the wards with quite a few broken hearts, Sharon suspected, but hers would never be one of them. He had asked her out numerous times, but although she liked him, she had always made some excuse, knowing that a date with Norton was bound to end in an undignified struggle. She had no wish to fall into such a trap, or to mislead him.

'Rose of Sharon . . . you're the pick of the bunch,' he said now, bestowing one of his charismatic, five-hundred-watt incandescent smiles on her, while she groaned at his pun. 'When are you coming out with me?' He stroked his fingers up and down her spine in a sensuous way.

'When you stop acting the fool,' she retorted, making

another vain attempt to get away from him.

His eyes narrowed a fraction. 'I'm not acting the fool. I'm deadly serious about you.'

Sharon was not sure whether the husky tone and smouldering eyes were contrived, or real. To her relief the lift stopped and the doors slid open, but at the same moment Norton, instead of releasing her as she expected, jerked her hard against him and kissed her with vigorous enthusiasm, his mouth crushing hers into submission and brooking no escape. Caught off guard Sharon was forced to endure it for a moment before she managed at last to wrench herself free of him, but by then it was too late to prevent the doors closing again. She was only in time to see, framed in the narrowing gap between them, and standing like a statue in the gleaming white corridor, Bryce Townshend. The look on his face was pure contempt, and it made her stomach turn over.

She beat her fists against Norton's chest. 'You stupid oaf, Norton! He saw! Now I'll get into a row . . . and one of these days you're going to be struck off!'

He smirked at her as the lift doors opened at the next floor. He patted her bottom playfully, and then ran a caressing hand across it. 'I'll bet he was jealous!' He gave her a triumphant look as he added, 'Cheers, sweetheart. Tell Sister I'll be down to tickle her fancy in a little while. She's been demanding my attention all day, poor frustrated old darling!'

He removed his hand from the doors and they closed, leaving Sharon fuming as she savagely pressed the button to return to her own floor. All the amused tolerance she normally had for the doctor and his antics had evaporated . . . and all because Bryce had seen her in a clinch with him. He was sure to report her to Sister and she would be bound to get a ticking off. She left the lift and went along to the cloakroom thinking angrily, 'Men!'

Hurriedly she changed out of her slacks and top into her crisp white uniform. In the corridor on her way to

Children's Surgical, she encountered one of the nurses going off duty.

Nurse Jean Watkins buttonholed her breathlessly. 'Sharon . . . watch it! The Gargoyle's on the war-path.'

'I know I'm a bit late . . .' Sharon said, her heart sinking.

Jean rolled her eyes heavenwards. 'It's not that. *He*'s been at her again.'

'*He?*'

'Dr Townshend! He tore a strip off her just now for something quite trivial . . . well, she said it was trivial. He was probably a bit uptight about Jamie Wilson.'

'Jamie . . . he's all right?' As Jean nodded, Sharon felt the terrible weakness of relief flooding through her, although she knew that just the fact that he had come through the operation was not necessarily cause for jubilation.

Jean smiled, a certain tenderness lighting her pretty vivacious features. 'He came through it all right, but he's not out of the wood yet by any means. The next few days are crucial. He's in intensive care, of course.'

'I'm glad,' Sharon murmured on another sigh of relief.

'So are we all,' said Jean with feeling. She added, 'I must fly, I've got a date tonight, rather a special one, and I want to buy a new dress!'

She fled, and Sharon braced herself for the encounter with the Gargoyle. Sister Garland would still be on duty for part of her shift since the rosters of sisters and nursing staff did not always coincide. She could imagine the glee with which Sister would tear a strip off her. If Dr Townshend had been reprimanding her she would be only too eager to vent her indignation on one of her nurses.

Sharon was therefore surprised when she glanced through the glass door of Sister Garland's office and the Gargoyle merely glanced up at her but did not call her in. Bryce had evidently not reported the incident right away as she had feared.

After the start-of-shift briefing, Sharon managed to look into the small intensive-care ward, adjacent to the main ward, where Jamie Wilson now lay. He was the only child there at the moment, and he was sleeping, his fair hair spread in a halo on the pillow. From the monitors she saw that his heartbeat and breathing were almost normal. She stood for a moment looking down at him, and around at the array of life-saving equipment to which the child was connected. Even now it sometimes seemed little short of miraculous to her that something so fragile and delicate as a human life could, even with the aid of sophisticated technology, survive. Life could snuff out so easily, yet it could also cling on tenaciously.

'Dr Townshend is hopeful of complete success this time,' the nurse on duty in the intensive-care ward informed Sharon.

Sharon smiled. 'That's good news.'

She worked her shift that afternoon and evening with a lighter heart. But all the time a small part of her mind kept returning to the enigmatic Dr Townshend, and she caught herself glancing up whenever someone entered the ward, half expectantly, half fearfully in case it was he.

There was no set visiting time for the parents of the children in Pinocchio so throughout the day mothers and fathers, grannies and aunts, came and went. Some stayed to play with their children or read to them, or help with some of the ward chores like feeding and bathing. Whenever she had a few free moments, Sharon would look for someone who needed cheering up a bit and either play a game with the child or read to him or her.

The ward itself, and the day-room, where those who were permitted out of bed during the day played, was decorated with colourful posters, and every effort was made to minimise the hospital appearance. At times the pace became rather hectic, but mostly there was a happy atmosphere, and Sharon, even when she felt totally exhausted at the end of a shift, always signed off and went home with a certain amount of exhilaration still clinging to her.

By the time she went up to the canteen for her tea break the ward was more or less quiet. Most of the younger children were already asleep, and Sharon had stopped glancing up every time someone came along the corridor or went into Sister's office, because she felt sure Bryce would have left the hospital by now.

In the canteen, another nurse, Erin Lucas, from Women's Surgical, joined Sharon.

'Pheeww!' she exclaimed, plonking her tray down on the table and falling into a chair. 'I feel whacked.' She pulled a face. 'Had a heavy night last night. What about you?'

'Oh . . . I went to a concert at the Town Hall,' said Sharon off-handedly.

'Who with?' Erin was always curious about everyone else's social life.

'Er . . . just a friend . . .' Sharon said, going a bit pink.

'Must be somebody special if you're keeping him dark,' said Erin pointedly. 'Somebody from South City?'

Sharon ignored her penetrating gaze and just shrugged and smiled noncommittally.

Fortunately Erin did not persist. Instead, she heaved a sigh and remarked, 'I reckon Dr Townshend must have had a heavy night too. He was on everyone's back like a plague of boils today.'

'Yes, Jean told me he was a bit scratchy,' said Sharon, stirring her coffee. 'He put the Gargoyle's back up apparently.'

'Not only her! You should have heard him blasting Sister Montrose, according to one of the nurses on my ward. I arrived just as he was leaving and the ward doors were swinging like a force nine gale had hit them. Montrose was practically apoplectic with fury.' She giggled suddenly. 'Know what she said?'

'No . . . tell me,' invited Sharon.

'Well, you know Montrose . . . she calls a spade a shovel every time. When I walked in there was a tide of crimson surging up her neck to her chin and she had her hands on those ample hips of hers and I thought she was going to have a seizure. She burst out, "What that man needs is a willing woman! Then he mightn't take out all his frustrations on us! He ought to get married!"'

Erin's accurate mimicry of Sister Montrose ended in laughter. At the same moment Sharon realised that someone was standing beside their table. She glanced up and was mortified to see Bryce Townshend, a tray in his hands. She felt the blood drain from her cheeks, and was aware that Erin, too, was horror-struck. He must have heard what she had said.

Erin recovered herself first. 'Oh, hello, Dr Townshend,' she said in a cheerful voice, that was obviously forced. She pushed her empty plates to one side, saying quickly, 'Excuse me . . . I've got to see someone in Pathology.' In another moment she was gone. Later she would be bound to be curious about what Dr Townshend was doing there anyway. Sharon was curious too.

Bryce said, 'Mind if I join you, Sharon? Or are you dashing off too?' He did not smile. His eyes were cold and accusing.

He's going to tell me off himself, Sharon thought. It was decent of him not to mention it to the Gargoyle, but it occurred to her that since he had, at the time, just had words with Sister, he might not have wanted to speak to her again, even by telephone. She steeled herself for what she thought was an inevitable dressing-down, and said, 'No, not for a minute or two.' She sipped her coffee nervously, not daring to look at him as he unloaded his tray.

It was unusual for one of the senior medical staff to mix with the nurses in the canteen. Some junior doctors and technicians did, but the surgeons tended to stick to that part of the dining room set aside for them. Sharon glanced around but no-one was looking curiously at them.

'You've seen Jamie?' Bryce inquired, propping his tray against the table leg.

Sharon risked a glance at him. 'Yes. But how is he . . . really?'

Bryce's eyes bored into hers, and seemed to be saying . . . or asking . . . things she could not translate, but which were patently different from the words coming out of his mouth. 'I think he'll be all right. He's a battler.'

'I hope so.' Sharon knew she sounded stiff, but she could not help it. She felt as though all her joints had suddenly locked.

'He'll be in intensive care for a few days.'

'Of course.'

There was a silence. Sharon felt inadequate, unable even to discuss Jamie Wilson's condition intelligently. She waited for Bryce to say something more about the operation but he just looked at her thoughtfully as she drank her coffee. He did not even mention Norton.

At length she said, 'I'd better get back.' She rose, wondering whether to say a few words about Jamie was after all the only reason he had come across to her table. It seemed that it was, but she was rather puzzled.

'Sharon . . .'

She faced him questioningly. Looking down at the smooth dark hair, the strong contours of his face, she knew a spine-tingling moment as she remembered as vividly as though it was happening again right now the feel of his lips on hers, warm, resilient, and masterful, so different from the brash, openly seductive embrace of Norton's. Norton was shallow. Bryce was deep, and Sharon knew without doubt which man she would rather have make love to her.

The thought brought a blush to her cheeks, but although his eyes held hers, they gave nothing away. A faintly cynical expression twisted his mouth as he shrugged and said, 'Nothing . . . good night.'

Dismissed, Sharon murmured good night and hurried out of the canteen. Had he meant to rebuke her and then changed his mind? Or didn't he think it important enough even to mention? There were plenty of others who wouldn't have turned a hair seeing her kissing Norton, but somehow she had expected Bryce to consider it very bad form on duty. Perhaps he hadn't realised it was her. The lift doors had closed swiftly. Then she recalled his look of contempt. He had known it was her.

'I bet you a Black Forest gateau he'll ask you out again,' declared Janna. She licked her lips. The cake was her favourite.

Sharon laughed. 'And you'll get to eat most of it whoever wins!'

'I still bet he will,' insisted Janna with conviction as she brushed her newly washed hair, while Sharon was busy ironing on the other side of the room.

'He hasn't yet,' said Sharon, 'and I bet you he won't.' It was now several days after her date with Dr Townshend.

'Why did he ask you in the first place?' demanded Janna stubbornly.

'I don't know. I suppose he had a reason. Or it was just a mad impulse, or curiosity, or a dare . . .'

'Rubbish!' said Janna flatly. 'And if he didn't make a pass at you and you didn't wallop him one . . . that is, if you've told the whole truth and nothing but the truth, he's bound to ask you out again.'

'I don't see why!' Sharon clattered the iron back on the stand and put the blouse she had been ironing on a hanger. 'Maybe it was just a whim . . . he had a spare ticket to the concert, he knew I liked Beethoven, and he thought it might be a bit of a giggle to take one of the nurses out, to flatter her ego.'

Janna turned around from the mirror and said in exasperation, 'Don't be so cynical! Men like Dr Townshend don't act on whims, or take up dares, and he's not the sort to get a kick out of flattering anyone's ego! He'll ask you again because he wants to . . . and maybe sooner than you think. He's just not the type to rush things.' She narrowed her eyes at Sharon. 'You want him to, don't you?'

Sharon coloured. 'I'm not sure that I do. I can't say I really enjoyed going out with him. I felt a bit uncomfortable.'

Janna laughed. 'Like dating royalty! I know what you mean. We poor underlings do tend to put the big noises on pedestals, but they're only human after all's said and done. Blood runs in their veins too. Of course, if you gazed at him in abject adoration all evening, he might have been a bit put off.'

'I did nothing of the kind!' retorted Sharon indignantly, thumping the iron down hard over a pair of jeans. 'I'm not a starry-eyed student nurse!'

Janna laughed as she pulled the bottom lids of her eyes down. 'Ugh . . . I ought to have half a dozen different fatal diseases by the look of my eyeballs. Incipient jaundice if nothing else.'

'Too much disco,' reproved Sharon teasingly, 'and not enough greens!'

Janna leapt up and gyrated to the beat of her own singing. When she collapsed into a chair, she said reflectively, 'I wonder why he's never married.'

'Who?'

'Townshend of course! Who else would I be talking about?'

Sharon did not want to discuss Bryce any more. 'I don't know and I don't think it would be something he'd talk about. I get the impression he's a very private person.'

'With a deep, dark, sensuous soul,' intoned Janna meaningfully, 'just waiting for a passionate, auburn-haired beauty to unlock its mysteries . . .'

'I'm going to make some coffee,' said Sharon, switching off the iron and moving the ironing board to one side.

She deliberately ignored what Janna had said. 'Want one?'

Janna chuckled. 'If that's a hint to stop talking about the handsome doctor, okay, but remember what I said . . .'

'A Black Forest gateau,' said Sharon dryly as she went out, 'I won't forget!'

During the next couple of weeks, Sharon saw Bryce many times, but he did not ask her out again. He was as cool and aloof as he had ever been and she was convinced now that he regretted having taken her to the concert, and probably regretted even more having kissed her afterwards. If anything there was more constraint between them than there had ever been. Every day Sharon insisted that Janna should buy the Black Forest gateau, but Janna refused.

'Give him time!' she always said gaily.

Sharon was not sure quite how she felt about it. She half wanted him to ask her out again—since it hurt her pride a little that he did not—but she also feared that he would, because she didn't know whether she wanted to accept or refuse.

One evening when she was off duty, she was sorting through her collection of records when she saw the Seventh Symphony, the Beethoven recording she had mentioned to Bryce and then forgotten about. He had said he would like to hear it. On an impulse she decided to take it in to him.

The next time he came into Pinocchio and there was no-one else in the offing, she casually mentioned it.

'I brought that Beethoven record in if you'd like to borrow it,' she offered.

His eyes met hers, puzzled, 'Record?'

She felt a bit foolish. He had forgotten of course, just as she had. At the time his interest had just been something to say. Now he would think her pushy for raising it. But she had to go on.

'I mentioned it . . . that night . . . we went to the concert, that I had a new recording of Beethoven's Seventh Symphony. You said you'd like to hear it. I remembered the other night when I was sorting out my records.'

His eyes did not blink, his face remained impassive. 'You've got it here?'

She nodded. 'That is, if you really want to hear it.'

He nodded briefly. 'Thank you . . . I'd like to.'

She fetched the recording and gave it to him. 'Keep it as long as you like,' she offered, regretting now that she had made the overture at all. She felt sure he was misinterpreting it, suspecting that she was attempting to initiate a relationship that he did not want. She wished she had not done such a stupid thing, and couldn't think why she had.

'I won't keep it long,' he promised. 'Thank you very much.'

A week passed and he did not return the record. Sharon did not dare to ask if he had listened to it yet, and what he thought of it. Every time he came into the ward, she endeavoured to occupy herself as far away from him as possible unless she specifically needed to consult him about a patient. For his part, he seemed as eager to avoid her, and certainly never sought her out. Sometimes, accidentally, they came face to face and always, after a moment of being caught by his unnerving gaze, Sharon found she was shaking.

One morning there was a worrying change in temperature of one of the children who was recovering from an operation to correct a ventricular septal defect, and Dr Townshend was called down to look at the patient, while the paediatrician who was doing the round was still in the ward.

Sharon was not needed, but her attention was inexorably drawn towards the group of the two doctors, and Sister Johnson who was on duty at the time, even though she was busy dressing one of the other small patients in a gown ready to go for an X-ray, meanwhile explaining reassuringly what was going to happen and what fun it would be.

In the middle of this she was startled by sudden piercing screams from the other side of the ward.

'Oh, no, not Lizbie again!' she groaned inwardly. The little three-year-old girl had only been in the ward for two days and had not adjusted at all well. It sometimes happened that no amount of soothing and reassuring and cuddling could pacify a child. Lizbie, who had fractured several ribs in a fall down some stairs, was just one of those children given to tantrums.

Sharon saw Jean Watkins rushing down the ward and at the same time was aware of Sister glancing round with a grim expression as though she expected her nurses to transport themselves at supersonic speed, and Dr Townshend and Dr Pearce also looking round, irritated at the interruption.

'Just wait a minute, darling,' Sharon said to the small boy she was attending to. 'I'll be right back.'

She sped after Jean to assist her in quietening Lizbie.

Jean groaned as she reached for the child, who straight away struggled and refused to be soothed. 'We'll have the whole lot screaming in a minute if she keeps up!'

Sharon knew it was not impossible for tantrums to be catching.

'Lizbie,' she pleaded, 'come on, love . . . what's the matter? Tell Sharon . . .'

'I hate you!' spat the child, screwing up her face ready for another scream.

'You'll hurt yourself,' said Sharon softly, 'and you wouldn't want to do that, would you? Come on, let's have a nice cuddle, shall we? Where's teddy? I'm sure he'd like a cuddle too.'

Jean said wryly, 'You're doing fine, Nurse! You've got the mother-touch. Shall I take young Simon to X-ray for you?'

'Yes, please.' Sharon had coaxed Lizbie into her arms and was gently smoothing the dark curls off her forehead and wiping the tears from the reddened cheeks. When the little girl had quietened, Sharon placed her back in her cot. Then she reached down to retrieve the teddy bear which Lizbie had hurled to the floor in her temper. 'Dear me,' she said in a very serious tone, 'poor teddy is hurt.'

'He's not,' said the child truculently.

'Indeed he is,' insisted Sharon. 'Look, you can feel he's broken some of his ribs. Just like you. That's what happens when people . . . and teddies . . . fall on the floor too hard.'

Lizbie followed Sharon's fingers and looked at her with interest. 'Poor teddy,' she said in a whisper.

Sharon knew she had won. She had aroused the child's sympathy for something else. 'What shall we do?' she asked. 'Shall we bandage him up until he gets better?'

'We'd better,' said Lizbie, very serious suddenly. She looked up at Sharon. 'Does he hurt too?'

'Oh yes, teddy hurts a lot,' said Sharon. 'You must be very careful with him. Now let me see, I think I might have a bandage in my pocket.'

Sharon's pockets tended to be full of surprising things and she remembered putting the end of a bandage in one earlier. She drew it out and with Lizbie watching intently, bound up teddy's chest. A moment later Lizbie was lying back on her pillow, crooning to her teddy bear, all signs of tantrum vanished.

'Well done, Nurse Derwent.'

Sharon turned around, startled, and swallowed hard as she saw Bryce standing at the end of the cot. She had not realised he was watching. She glanced quickly along the ward. Sister and Dr Pearce were at the other end talking.

'You have a sure touch,' Bryce said, and there was a softness in his eyes that Sharon suddenly wished could be for her, not just for a sick child.

'Lizbie is a bit of a problem,' she said straightening up, 'but for the moment at least she's more concerned about teddy than herself.'

Bryce glanced at the child and the toy. A smile flitted across his face. 'You obviously did a stint in Casualty some time,' he remarked.

'Yes . . .' Then Sharon realised that he was teasing because of the bandaged bear. She smiled ruefully.

There was an uncomfortable moment of silence, during which he still stood there motionless, watching as she tidied up a few scattered objects, waiting for him to go away.

At last he said, 'I would like a word with you, Nurse Derwent, if you can spare a moment.'

'Of course . . .' Her heart was hammering. What could he want to say? Some criticism no doubt. She said, as they walked to the end of the ward, 'What did you want to speak to me about, Dr Townshend?'

He paused. They were alone for the moment. Sister was back in her office and Dr Pearce had gone. Sharon felt the colour rushing into her cheeks as he surveyed her with a searching gaze. She looked away. She still felt foolish about the record and wished he would hurry up and give it back and then she could forget all about it.

His voice fractured her thoughts. 'What about this weekend?'

Her eyes flicked back to his face. 'W . . . weekend?' she stammered, not understanding.

A fleeting smile curved his lips. He was amused at her incomprehension. 'You're off duty on Sunday, aren't you?'

'Ye-es . . .'

'I thought we might ride somewhere . . . have a picnic . . .'

Sharon almost collapsed in a heap in the middle of the ward floor. 'You . . . you mean on bicycles?' she said.

His eyes held hers challengingly. 'That is, if you want to come.'

She knew she ought to say no, but she said recklessly, 'Yes . . . I'd like to . . . Thank you.'

'Good,' he answered with his usual directness and brevity of speech. 'I'll call round on Sunday about nine.' A faint glimmer of a smile flickered across his face again. 'Too early for you?'

'No, I always get up early . . . except when I've been on nights, of course.'

'See you then,' he said, and was gone before Sharon had time to marshall her scattered wits, consider what had just occurred, and realise that she had committed herself, though whether wisely or not she could not at that moment decide.

Janna, of course, was jubilant when she discovered where Sharon was going on Sunday.

'I told you,' she chortled. 'Don't forget you owe me . . .'

'. . . a Black Forest gateau,' said Sharon dryly. 'It's already ordered!'

CHAPTER THREE

JANNA did not come in until the early hours of Sunday morning, so when it was time for her to get up, Sharon crept about very quietly so as not to disturb her. Not that anything short of an earthquake usually did disturb Janna when she was deeply asleep.

At a quarter to nine, Sharon was ready to go. She realised that they had not come to any arrangement about who was to provide what for the picnic, so she made enough sandwiches and tea for two in case Bryce was expecting her to. He was the kind of man, she decided, who would expect it. She still felt rather bemused by the second invitation, and as she had on the night of the concert, a little nervous. It was so long since that night that today's outing was almost like a first one.

Tying a scarf gipsy fashion around her hair, which she had bunched into a pony-tail, and rolling up the bottoms of her jeans, Sharon slipped quietly out of the flat. Leaving the picnic lunch near the entrance, she wheeled her bicycle out of the store-room. She was pumping up the tyres when the loud ringing of a bell startled her. Bryce had arrived.

He looked totally different this morning. Not at all like the aloof and sometimes irritable Dr Townshend, or like the rather suave concert-goer. He too was wearing jeans, topped with a plain white T-shirt, almost the same as her own. He looked much younger than usual, she thought. He laughed outright when he saw her similar outfit.

'Hello there! This must be the fashionable rig for biking!'

Sharon smiled. She felt warm and happy suddenly,

quite the opposite of what she had expected. 'Hello,' she said.

He dismounted and stood looking at her. 'I must say it looks better on you!' he commented, as his eyes drifted flatteringly over her shapely figure. The tight jeans emphasised her lissom thighs and long legs, and the T-shirt clung revealingly to her firm rounded breasts. 'Nurses' uniforms don't do a lot for the female figure, do they?'

Sharon, blushing uncomfortably under this frank appraisal, clipped the pump back in place and said as nonchalantly as she was able, 'Well, I'm ready.' She loaded the bag containing the picnic lunch into the wire basket behind the saddle and clipped the strap securely over to hold it. She noticed that Bryce also had what must be lunch in his front basket, after all.

He said, 'I thought we wouldn't waste our energy on polluted highways but take the train to Lilydale and meander about from there.'

'Sounds a good idea,' Sharon agreed, feeling suddenly that the day might prove enjoyable after all.

On the train Bryce seemed so much more relaxed than she had so far found him, that she began to forget he was Dr Townshend. He was just another cycling enthusiast, and in fact much more of one than she had ever been. He spent most of the journey telling her about cycling tours he had done in Europe and also in Thailand. He was something of a raconteur, she discovered, to her delight, and several times had her rocking with laughter at the incidents that had befallen him.

It was a warm sunny day, but the sun was not unbearably hot and there was a light breeze, perfect for leisurely cycling. Sharon was content to let Bryce decide the direction they would take, and as it was the first time for ages she had been far outside the city, she felt exhilarated in the traffic-free side roads he led her along, and the fresh unpolluted air. It was air to sharpen the appetite and after an hour or so Bryce said:

'Lunch time, I think, don't you?'

He turned off along a side track that presently took them over a wooden bridge, through yellow-brown paddocks and into the bush. Beyond, the hills were deep misty blue against the paler blue of the sky, and quite close to them now.

'Just near here is a favourite spot of mine,' Bryce said, as he dismounted and they continued on foot, wheeling their bicycles along a sandy track to the creek bank. 'I used to live near Lilydale when I was young, so I know the area quite well.'

'It's very peaceful,' said Sharon, with a contented sigh.

Near the creek they came to a grassy clearing surrounded by gum trees and casuarinas and acacias. Rosellas flashed blue and crimson in the sunshine as they fled at the sudden human intrusion, then perched high in the trees, whistling and screeching. A solitary brown cow eyed them superciliously over a fence.

'Mmm . . . this is perfect,' said Sharon, propping her bike against a tree. 'Just what the tired mind and body needs.'

Bryce studied her for a long moment, half smiling. 'Yes . . .' he drawled, and Sharon had the uncomfortable feeling that they were not necessarily talking about the same thing.

They stretched out on a patch of grass and spent the next little while devouring the sandwiches Sharon had brought and the cold pie Betsy had provided, all washed down with hot tea from both their thermoses, and finishing with crisp Grannie Smith apples, Betsy's final and welcome contribution. Only a small portion of pie remained that neither could manage.

Bryce laughed, and leaning back on his elbows said with satisfaction, 'I think we did that lot fair justice!'

Sharon patted her stomach and groaned. 'I feel such a pig! I never eat so much! But Betsy's pie was delicious.'

'She's a good cook,' he said. 'She looks after me too

well, really. She spoils me. She was with my parents for years, and she's really like one of the family.' He slid a sly, teasing look at Sharon. 'You could carry a bit more flesh without spoiling the outlines! That's the trouble with you girls living away from home, you don't know how to eat properly.'

'Are you going to lecture me?' she demanded, with a smile.

'No.'

They relaxed in silence again for some minutes. It was perfect, Sharon thought, just sitting there, companionably, watching the sluggish creek winding between the stones and flood debris of branches and mud, cool under the canopy of leaves through which the sun flickered in a dappled pattern of light. Here the silence was truly golden, broken only by the double whistle of the crimson rosellas calling to each other in the treetops as they fed on the nuts left from the previous flowering of the gum blossom, and the strident vibrations of a cicada or cricket, warmed into a response to the sun.

Once or twice their eyes met, and each half-smiled. Sharon felt a warmth flowing through her that had nothing to do with the heat of the day. Once she said something about the hospital and Bryce reached across to lay a finger on her lips.

'No shop,' he rebuked gently. 'You must learn to leave it all behind sometimes.'

For the first time Sharon looked really deeply into his eyes and saw that the grey was flecked with a lighter colour, blue, and that his lashes were longer and lusher than any she had seen on a man.

'Sorry,' she apologised, looking quickly away, because the intensity of his gaze disconcerted her.

He chuckled. 'I suppose it's an occupational hazard. We do tend to live and breathe our kind of jobs.'

'You can't really detach yourself completely,' Sharon agreed.

He sighed. 'Some can. It all depends whether you

regard it as a job or a vocation, I suppose.' He sat up abruptly and slapped a hand against his thigh. 'But I said no shop!' He turned to look speculatively at her. 'What do you usually do in your spare time?'

Sharon shrugged. 'Sleep!'

'Not all the time!'

'No. I shop and clean and wash and iron and gossip with Janna. We go dancing, to the theatre sometimes. I read when I get time.' She looked at him apologetically. 'A pretty ordinary life really.' And then boldly, 'What do you do?'

He had turned sideways so that he was looking at her while resting his head on his hand, supported on his elbow. 'I go to concerts and the theatre. I don't dance much, I'm afraid. I haven't got much sense of rhythm. I play golf when I can. It's very relaxing. Have you ever played?'

'No, but my father does,' said Sharon. 'That is when he can get down to Melbourne, or he's on holiday.'

'Your parents don't live in Melbourne?' Bryce queried.

'No. I come from a small town in northern Victoria. Winnabri. I came down to Melbourne to do my training, and here I've stayed.' She added, 'But we do have a very good bush nursing hospital in Winnabri.'

'Are your parents farmers?' he inquired.

'No. Dad's a local GP,' Sharon explained.

His eyebrows rose. 'I see. So medicine is in the family. Like mine. My mother was a doctor, and two of my uncles. Quite a rash of medicos actually. Myself and two cousins in the younger generation, and now my brother's oldest is talking about doing medicine.'

It was the first time he had said anything about his own family.

Sharon said, 'I've got two brothers. One's in forestry and the other's still at university in Canberra. He's going to be a lawyer. No doctors I'm afraid.' She added casually, not wanting to sound too curious, 'You said your mother . . . was a doctor.'

He nodded. 'She died a couple of years ago. Dad's been dead for twenty years. He was a cellist . . . oh, nobody famous or anything like that. He played in the State orchestra. She met him in England when she was studying there. A whirlwind romance, but a successful one.' As he spoke his lips curled ironically.

Sharon wondered about his own relationship with the woman he had mentioned only once, and longed to ask him about her, but dared not because she knew he would think her impertinent. He would close up immediately and the easy-going atmosphere that now existed between them would instantly dissipate if he thought she was prying.

There was another long silence, and for a moment Sharon thought he must have gone to sleep. He had stretched out full length on the grass, and was lying very still, his hands clasped behind his head, his eyes closed. Sharon studied his face. In repose it was gentler, and there was a softness not usually noticeable in the stern straightness of his nose, the strong jawline, the determined mouth, that betrayed his capacity for compassion. There were pairs of small lines bracketing his lips, others fanning out almost imperceptibly below and at the corners of his eyes, and deep creases from his nose to his chin. He was probably in his late thirties, Sharon thought.

An ant ran up his neck onto his cheek but he did not stir. Sharon noticed and moved slightly to bend over him as she flicked the insect off as lightly as she could to avoid waking him. He may not have felt the ant, but he felt the light touch of her fingers and his eyes flicked open. For a long moment his eyes melted into hers, and she said in a strange, croaked sort of voice. 'There was an ant . . . crawling on your face . . .'

He did not answer but lifted his arms and purposefully folded them around her, drawing her down on top of him. One hand moved to the back of her head, his fingers raking through her hair as he guided her lips to his, raising his own head slightly to crush her mouth in a kiss that drew deeply on the well of her responses, and banished any resolve she might have had to resist him.

She did not resist either when his hand deftly pulled her T-shirt free of the waistband of her jeans and his warm fingers explored her skin, moving tantalisingly up and down her spine, finding and caressing sensitive places, and then more boldly he cradled her against one arm while seeking fingers pushed her flimsy bra out of the way so that he could cup and caress the firm roundness of her breasts. His lips parted from hers for a moment and his eyes bored deeply into hers. A faint smile creased his whole face and desire hung, barely controlled, in his smouldering eyes.

'You are so very nice, Sharon,' he whispered, and changed position slightly so that his long hard body pressed down on hers. His legs gripped her tightly and his mouth communicated his mounting desire.

Sharon responded with an eagerness she knew she might well later feel ashamed of, but could not deny then. Her hands clasped his neck and dragged his lips down hard onto hers. It was as though something had kindled a fire inside her which had never been lit before, and the warmth of it flowed through her veins like an injection of some drug designed to give instant well-being.

How long they might have remained, locked in each other's arms, fused in a kiss that neither wanted to break, Sharon never knew, because all at once the sound of a car engine and voices disturbed the peace and tranquillity, causing them to jerk apart guiltily, sit up and look around. A party of picnickers had parked their car at the edge of the clearing and were coming down the slope carrying rugs, and chairs, and plastic cool-boxes, and making a great deal of noise doing it. They were evidently going to settle to a late lunch.

Bryce glanced ruefully at Sharon. 'Let's go,' he said

briefly, an expression of distaste on his face.

Sharon stood up, brushing bits of grass and dust from her clothes, pulling her hair back and re-fastening it with the pony-tail clip. She was aware that she must look a mess, and she was afraid to meet Bryce's eyes. He brushed her back down, and she did the same for him, both actions causing her to experience a fresh rush of the electrifying feeling he had already aroused in her.

They picked up the remains of their picnic, and slowly made their way back to where they had left their bicycles. Sharon felt a deep sense of loss, as though what had happened had been a dream and she had woken up too soon. But the sensible side of her insisted that the interruption had probably been timely.

Bryce said nothing except, 'Time we headed back anyway.'

They rode slowly, savouring the afternoon as the shadows began to lengthen, and eventually arrived back at the station just as a train was arriving. They did not talk as much on the return journey as they had on the train going out. Sharon wondered what Bryce was thinking, but he gave her no clue.

At Flinders Street, he suddenly said, 'You don't have to rush home yet, do you?'

A little taken aback, since she had expected them to part company there, she said, 'No . . .'

'Then let's go up to my place. We can have a cup of tea in peace and quiet and I can give you back your record.'

Sharon hesitated. 'It's getting late . . .'

'I'll drive you home afterwards,' he said at once. 'We can stow your bike in the boot.'

'Can we . . .?' She was thinking of the sleek grey Mercedes. Had he ever tried it before?

He read her thoughts. 'I've done it myself on occasions.'

'All right,' Sharon agreed, not knowing how to get out of it now, and not really wanting to, although she wondered, in view of what had happened earlier, whether it was wise.

Within a few minutes they were at his house, and Sharon was again walking into the elegant drawing room and looking about her with delight and a little envy. It would be wonderful to live in such a house, she thought wistfully.

'What did you think of the recording?' she asked.

Bryce was standing by uncertainly, as though he had forgotten why they were there. 'Recording . . .?' He seemed to jerk out of some reverie he had slipped into. 'Yes . . . the recording . . . I enjoyed it very much. Quite excellent in fact. One of the best interpretations I've heard.' He continued to look at her as though weighing up something in his mind, and his scrutiny made Sharon feel ill at ease once more.

'I'll make that cup of tea,' he said abruptly. 'It's Betsy's day off.'

Sharon followed him out to the kitchen this·time. It was smaller than she had expected, modern in all its appurtenances, but with a touch of elegance in its decor. There was pine panelling on the walls, and a great deal of shining copper and brass. Here too the colour scheme was brown and beige with touches of orange and yellow, but the muted background tones were more soothing than monotonous.

Bryce glanced at the clock. 'I could rustle up a bit of a scratch meal,' he said, with a questioning look, and, she thought, as though he wanted her to say yes.

'We could warm up that piece of pie we didn't eat,' she suggested.

He was peering into the refrigerator. 'Plenty of cheese, eggs, mushrooms . . . can you make omelettes?'

'Yes . . .'

He grinned at her. 'I'm very fond of mushroom omelettes.'

Sharon said, 'All right, but what about the pie?'

He dismissed it abruptly. 'That'll do for Rusty.'

'Who's Rusty?'

'Betsy's dog. She'll have taken him with her. She's gone to her sister's at Frankston for the weekend. Rusty likes the beach. Do you like large shaggy hounds?' he inquired with a laugh.

'I love all dogs,' she answered, and was warmed by his look of approval.

So they skipped having a cup of tea, and had a meal instead. While Sharon sautéed the mushrooms, finely chopped with some parsley she had found in the crisper and a spring onion, and mixed the eggs, Bryce set two places at the breakfast bar (at Sharon's insistence since she felt it would be a shame to disturb the dining room), opened a bottle of white wine, and put a pot of coffee on to percolate. He also put a couple of records on the stereo, first some Mozart which Sharon enjoyed, and then one of her favourites, the Trout Quintet by Schubert, while they were eating.

Later Bryce changed the atmosphere completely by putting some moody modern music on the turntable, and seeing Sharon's surprised look as she carried the coffee into the drawing room, he said, 'Just to prove I'm not a complete square!'

They sat side by side on the couch and Sharon poured the coffee. She felt totally at ease with him now. He was so different when you got to know him, she reflected, and smiling privately added silently—so nice.

She gazed around her and sighed contentedly. 'I love this room. Did you have a hand in choosing the decor, Bryce, or did you just let interior decorators interpret your personality?' She smiled at him a little teasingly.

That she had inadvertently touched a raw nerve was immediately obvious. He tensed and there was a small charged silence before he answered abruptly, 'No, I didn't have much hand in it. Naomi took charge of the redecoration, but it reflects my taste too.' He added casually, 'Naomi was the woman I once lived with.'

Sharon regretted her remark, and there was nothing she could say after his reply. A sidelong glance at him showed her that it was a subject he did not want to discuss. After a moment, however, he went on:

'It was some years ago.' He seemed to be making a point of the distance in time as though to assure her that the past was buried.

There was still nothing she felt she could safely say, and she wished she had not innocently crashed into his private life. The easier, more relaxed atmosphere had vanished and Sharon felt strongly that the tension was mounting with every minute. Unwittingly she had spoiled the evening.

At last she said, 'I think I'd better be going. I'm on early shift for a few weeks.' She added tentatively, 'What about the washing up?'

'Betsy will be furious if there's nothing for her to do tomorrow,' he said. 'She expects me to make a mess!'

It was lightly said, but there were shadows behind his eyes, and Sharon knew she had blundered by making him recall Naomi. There was a pulse beating rapidly in his neck and he looked tense.

When she rose, he did too, and she thought ruefully, he's glad to get rid of me now. But he stood very close to her, looking down at her as though he meant to say something, but although his lips moved, no words came out. He slipped his arms around her and drew her against him, and Sharon did nothing to prevent it. She wasn't expecting it, but she wasn't surprised. It seemed quite natural. For a few moments his fingers played idly with strands of her hair, and then he unclipped the pony-tail clasp and let the thick tresses fall about her shoulders.

'Sharon . . .' He said her name softly, but with an eagerness that made her tremble. His fingers traced the shape of her ears and explored the slender curve of her neck and throat, before he bent his head and kissed her. Then again he murmured more urgently, 'Sharon . . .' as he lifted his head and looked into her eyes, desire clearly stated in his. 'You don't know how much I've wanted to do this . . .'

'Bryce . . .' she mumbled foolishly, not knowing what to say.

'You've been tantalising me for a very long time,' he said, drawing her hard against him. 'Every time I saw you in the ward, I wanted you . . . I couldn't keep my eyes off you . . . I wanted to close my fingers around that tiny waist . . .' He did so, laughing to see that his fingers and thumbs almost met. 'I wanted to kiss those ever-smiling generous lips . . . feel your body warmly breathing against mine . . . Don't look so astonished! The grizzly bear is a man underneath, you know!'

Sharon did know. She had had a taste of it one night several weeks ago, and just how much of a man she had begun to learn that afternoon. But deep inside her a warning voice said she was a fool to get involved, that it would be the quickest way to get hurt.

But the warning voice was faint when he crushed her roughly in his arms and kissed her with passion even more explosive than earlier down by the creek. Sharon's senses reeled as she felt herself filling with the same fiery glow once more, and knew that this time she would be consumed, and would not be able to help it.

But even as her lips parted against his and her fingers raked through his hair, a sudden icy draught killed the fire flaring up so dangerously inside her. From the depths of her subconscious came Erin's voice, telling her what Sister Montrose had said. Sharon had forgotten her words until now, but suddenly they had a chilling significance. 'What that man needs is a willing woman', Sister Montrose had said. 'Then he might not take out all his frustrations on us.'

Bryce had most probably heard what Erin had said. And he must have decided she would be a willing woman. Burning with shame and anger, Sharon wrenched herself away from him, springing across the room as though hurled by an electric shock. All he was doing was following Sister Montrose's advice.

'I'm sorry,' Sharon said coldly, maintaining her calm with a super-human effort. 'I must have misled you . . . I'm not the kind of person you want. I don't believe in casual affairs.'

She should never have come back with him, she thought. She should have known the danger after what had happened this afternoon. What sort of naive fool was she? Or had she thought . . . that his intentions were different. That, she told herself bitterly, made her an even bigger fool.

Bryce looked utterly astonished at her outburst, and did not move for a moment. Then he started across the room towards her. Sharon, giving in to a sudden blind panic, dashed frantically around the obstructing furniture, gained the door to the hallway, and was about to fling open the front door when a vice-like grip on her wrist prevented her from doing so.

He whirled her round to face him, and she stared into his face, distraught, and terrified. She was a fool, she told herself wildly, a stupid fool, and she was going to get what she deserved.

'Let me go,' she cried desperately, 'oh, please let me go! I don't want to . . .'

To her immense surprise he was chuckling softly, as without any undue effort he wrapped his arms around her and imprisoned her slight frame against his implacable solidity so that she had no hope of escape. Her chin pressed hard against his breast bone.

'You silly little goose,' he murmured, 'I'm not going to rape you, or even seduce you . . . I want to *marry* you!'

A deathly hush fell across the hallway, which a moment ago had resounded to Sharon's desperate pleas. She stood rigidly imprisoned in his arms, stunned beyond belief. She could feel her heart hammering fit to burst out of her ribcage, and her ears still burned with the echo of his astonishing words.

'Marry me?' she whispered at last, searching his face for mockery, for deception, the shadows of fear still lurking in her own.

'Yes my sweet Sharon, marry you . . .' He tilted her chin and laid a featherlight kiss on her trembling lips. 'Is that so strange? Come along, let's go back into the drawing room and sit down and talk about it. I had meant to lead up to it a little less violently.' He was smiling as he released her. He patted her cheeks swiftly but lightly with the palms of his hands. 'I do believe you're in a state of shock! A small brandy is called for, I think.'

Mutely, Sharon followed him back into the drawing room, and zombie-like allowed him to guide her to the couch, sit her down gently, fetch them both a brandy, and then take his place beside her. He watched while she sipped the brandy and there was amusement dancing in his eyes.

Sharon put her glass down, her hands still trembling, and let the fiery liquid course through her. It brought a welcome feeling of relaxation almost at once. Then she looked at Bryce.

'I'm sorry . . . I behaved like a fool.'

He reached for her hand and held it as tenderly in his as though it were an injured bird to be handled with extreme care.

'No, I was the one who behaved like a fool. I did it all wrong. I never was much good at the niceties of romance . . .' He gave her a rueful look and ran his other hand through his hair as he sighed regretfully. 'I hope you'll forgive me.' His gaze was very earnest. 'Will you?'

'I . . . I'm too stunned to do anything,' Sharon said shakily. 'I don't understand . . .'

Bryce clasped her hand very tightly between both of his. 'I'm asking you to marry me, Sharon. Will you?'

The directness of his gaze seemed to belie that it was a joke, but he couldn't mean it . . . could he? Sharon was convinced that she must be either dreaming or he was drunk. But she had been with him all day and he had drunk only a little over half a bottle of wine, that was all.

He was as sober as she was. So he must be mad.

'But you don't know me,' she muttered. 'We've only been out together twice . . .'

'I've known you for a year.'

'Yes, but . . .' She faltered, feeling that this was an argument she was bound to lose on grounds of logic. 'But we don't know anything about each other, Bryce. We only know each other professionally. Besides . . .'

'Besides what?' His grey eyes glittered challengingly.

Sharon looked away and said in a barely audible voice, 'You're a senior surgeon. I'm just a staff nurse.'

'And what has that got to do with it?' he demanded, in the voice that made nurses, other doctors and anyone who contradicted him quail.

Sharon glanced back at him, her lips pursed. 'Everything . . . and you know it.' She flung her hands out helplessly. 'We . . . we live in different worlds.' Her quick glance around the room confirmed it.

He ignored her protest. 'Sharon, we're two people very much attracted to each other—you can't deny that —and so far as I'm concerned, that's all that matters.'

Sharon stared at their intertwined hands, then Bryce slid closer and pulled her against him, tucking her head under his chin.

'I dare you to say you're indifferent to me,' he whispered, nuzzling her hair, and bending his lips to nibble her ear. 'You can't deny that we set each other alight.'

'No . . . but . . .' Sister Montrose's words still rang in her ears.

'Now what's your objection?' he said impatiently.

'It's just that it's so sudden,' Sharon said weakly.

Marriage! Dr Townshend was the last person she would ever have expected a proposal from. There was no doubt that he had aroused her emotions, kindled her desires in a way no other man had done, but would she be wise to marry him?'

Bryce turned her face up to his and kissed her lips provocatively. 'Don't think about it too long, Sharon.

I'm not a very patient man.'

Sharon averted her face. 'Marriage is a big step. Bryce, it's not . . . well it's not quite the same as just living together. You can end that any time.'

His fingers stroked the back of her neck and applied an arousing pressure to her nape. 'You said you didn't want a casual affair. Nor do I.'

She turned quickly to look into his face, to try to catch the truth there, and failed. He was simply smiling at her. She said lamely, 'Why do you want to get married?'

He did not answer directly. 'You're worried because I told you I once lived with another woman, aren't you? I suppose I had better tell you about her.'

'You don't have to . . .' Sharon protested, but she was burning to hear it.

'We can't have her shadow between us,' Bryce said, 'so here's the story, very briefly, and then I hope we won't have to mention it again. It's a part of my life I prefer to forget.' He took a deep breath and resolutely went on, 'I was newly qualified and Naomi was half way through her course.'

'She was a doctor too?' Sharon interrupted.

'Yes. Eventually. We decided to live together because we . . . well she believed in independence. She didn't want children. She was determined to get to the top in her field—like me she had chosen surgery and wanted to specialise in cardiology. We lived together for two years. I bought this house with the legacy from my father, the interest from which had already seen me through medical school, and despite the lack of vows I naively imagined we would stay together. At first while she was still training we were happy, but once she qualified it began to turn sour. Perhaps the mistake was our both being in the same field. I don't know, but she walked out one day and went to live with someone else.'

Sharon glanced at him with sympathy, but said nothing.

There was a growing tension in his voice as he continued his story. 'It was a blow, but as we were not married there were no ghastly formalities necessary to make the severance final. She went abroad some time later, to America. Eventually I went overseas too. That was when I worked in hospitals in Europe and Asia, and did my bicycling tours.' He glanced down at her with a smile. 'Nothing like a long bike ride to clear one's head, is there?'

'Did she marry the man she left you for?' asked Sharon, a wave of anguish for him washing over her.

'I really don't know. I rarely see any of her friends now, and the one or two people who would know tactfully do not mention her to me.'

'Is . . . she still in America?' Sharon asked.

He hesitated for a moment, then said hastily, 'Yes, I imagine so.'

Sharon said, 'I still don't understand why, after such an experience, you want to marry me.'

'I'm the marrying kind,' he answered briefly.

Sharon was momentarily disappointed. She realised she had hoped that he would say he loved her.

He toyed with her fingers. 'Sharon . . . I'm sorry if I was clumsy . . . if I got a bit carried away today, both out there in the bush, and a few minutes ago, but you don't know how much I've wanted to hold you in my arms.'

Sharon felt her heart melting, but Sister Montrose's reported words persisted in echoing in her head, '. . . and then he might not work off his frustrations on us!' She had also said, according to Erin, 'He ought to get married!'

He was in his late thirties. No doubt a lot of people said it was about time he got married. Perhaps he was sick of hearing them say it, so he had picked on her at random, confident that any of the nurses would fall over themselves with eagerness to become Mrs Bryce Townshend. But why had he waited so long? The obvious answer was disillusionment, or perhaps he still loved Naomi?

He was still speaking. 'I admit that if you had allowed it, things might have got out of hand just now.' He tilted her face up to his again, and his eyes were smiling, not a vestige of deceit lurking anywhere in them. Or did she not want to see it? He said, 'I'm a red-blooded man after all, despite the white coat and stethoscope, and the necessarily biological approach to the human body.' He chuckled. 'Your body, my dear Sharon, has the distinct tendency to chase any thought of biology from my mind, and set my red corpuscles in complete disarray.'

'How do I know this isn't just an act to get me into bed?' Sharon said bluntly. 'And in a week or two when you're bored with me you'll say it was all a mistake and the engagement is off?'

His hurt look was very convincing. 'Sharon! Is that what you think of me? Do you really believe I would stoop to such a ruse—or that I would . . .' He paused and she knew that only modesty had stopped him from saying 'would have to'. It was doubtless true. He had enough charisma to tempt a woman into bed without asking her to marry him.

'I don't know what to think,' she answered honestly.

He drew her close in an affectionate squeeze. 'Sharon, I promise I will never lose control of myself with you, until we are married. I promise we will never go further than you want to. If you wish it, we will not even risk our emotions by being alone together after this evening until our wedding night. Is that evidence enough of my *bona fides*?'

'You make me feel like a prude,' she said sheepishly.

He kissed the top of her head. 'I'm sure you are not.' There was a lengthy pause during which his chin rested on her head and she could feel his heart beating steadily. Then he said, 'Well, Sharon? What is your answer?'

The overwhelming desire to say yes right then was almost victorious, but Sharon suppressed it, and said half apologetically, 'Bryce . . . I . . . I'll have to think about it.'

CHAPTER FOUR

As Sharon expected, Janna was eager to hear about her day's outing with Bryce at the weekend. There was no avoiding the inquisition.

'How did it go?' Janna asked, cutting a slice of her Black Forest gateau with some relish.

'Fine,' Sharon answered airily.

'Oh, come on,' urged Janna, 'don't be a meanie. What happened?'

Sharon composed her face, then announced deadpan, 'He asked me to marry him!'

Janna dropped the slice of cake. It fell into a squashy lump on the plate. 'He what?' she squeaked.

'He asked me to marry him.' Sharon could not help a little mischievous enjoyment at the expense of her friend. She had known that Janna would be as dumb-founded as she was herself.

Janna recovered herself more quickly however. 'Well, didn't I say he fancied you,' she said gleefully. 'When's the wedding going to be? I hope I'm going to be a bridesmaid.'

'I haven't actually said yes, yet.' Although she was making light of it, Sharon was inwardly in turmoil.

Janna's blue eyes widened in amazement. 'Good grief! You mean you didn't snap him up on the spot. What's the matter with you?'

'I . . . I'm not sure . . . I mean, I hardly know him,' Sharon said doubtfully.

Janna crammed cake into her mouth, chewed and swallowed before she exclaimed again, 'What are you talking about? You've received a proposal of marriage from the most eligible bachelor in South City General, probably in the whole of the Melbourne medical profession, and you're dithering!'

'You wouldn't marry Peter unless you were in love with him, would you?' Sharon asked.

Janna rolled her eyes. 'That's quite different. Peter is a mere medical equipment salesman. Dr Townshend is a senior surgeon and an eminent cardiologist. There's no comparison. You don't turn down proposals of marriage from the likes of him!' She grinned. 'If he'd asked me, I'd be doing cartwheels!'

'You, Janna Wills, are a blatant materialist,' rebuked Sharon with a laugh. 'I hope Peter realises it.'

'I'm working on it!' Janna said wickedly. She eyed the cake and rubbed her stomach. 'I really shouldn't have any more . . . well, perhaps just a sliver . . .'

'You can't cut slivers of that sort of cake,' Sharon pointed out.

They exchanged glances. 'Oh, well,' said Janna with a grin, 'the first day of my diet starts tomorrow.' She cut another ample wedge, and looked seriously at Sharon. 'Don't worry, you're more than half way in love with him. I can tell. You've got that swept-off-your-feet look about you. You're just a bit dumbfounded at the moment.'

'I know,' Sharon admitted. She reached for a few crumbs of the luscious rich confection that Janna was purposefully demolishing. 'But how do I know it isn't just his position, his beautiful house, his Mercedes . . . tempting me?'

'Don't be so moral!' expostulated Janna. 'Anyway, you must have some clue how you feel about him. Come on, tell . . . what does it feel like when he kisses you? Do you go all melting and funny peculiar inside?'

Sharon blushed as she recollected Bryce's kisses. 'I wouldn't describe it quite like that.'

'Do you want to leap into bed with him?' asked Janna bluntly.

Sharon's colour deepened. 'That's only physical . . .'

Janna hugged herself gleefully. 'You do! Well, that's a good sign. Never marry a man you don't want to go to bed with. That's bound to cause trouble. Now, let's see, what have you got in common besides healing the sick? You both like riding bicycles . . .' She giggled uncontrollably for a few seconds. 'It sounds almost kinky! What else? You enjoy classical music . . . come on, Sharon, you must have talked about something.'

'We . . . we both like children,' admitted Sharon. She had been listing things in her mind ever since Bryce had brought her home last night, and she had lain awake feeling that she must be dreaming. 'Well, I think we like the same kinds of food . . . and oriental things . . . and dogs . . .'

'Enough,' pronounced Janna. 'You've got everything, including your profession, in common. Sharon Derwent, if you don't say yes to Bryce Townshend, you need your head examined. You'll never find a more compatible partner. Don't you realise it all adds up to love?'

Sharon smiled ruefully. She wished sometimes that she could think in such a cut and dried, black and white way as Janna did. 'Yes, I suppose it does. That's what I've been telling myself. It's just that . . .' She shrugged. She was not sure what it was that was making her hesitate. 'I don't know, perhaps I'm just being ultra cautious. It's a big step to take.'

'Chicken out,' warned Janna, 'and I warrant you'll regret it for the rest of your life. Tell him yes tomorrow, right? Promise, Sharon?'

Sharon did not answer. She had another night to sleep on it. Tomorrow evening Bryce was taking her out to dinner and she had a feeling he would press her for an answer then. It would not be fair to keep him waiting too long.

The wedding ceremony was held in the garden of Bryce's house, beneath the shade of a spreading jacaranda in the rear garden. Sharon felt more nervous than she had ever felt in her life. Standing beside Bryce, with the breeze lifting her veil playfully, and catching his eye as he glanced at her while the Reverend Coates intoned the vows, she had a dreadful feeling in the pit of her stomach that it was all wrong, that she ought not to have committed herself—or him.

She experienced a moment of panic, but there was no escape now. She was being asked to say 'I do' and 'I will' and in a wavering voice she was repeating the vows, promising to love, honour and . . . yes . . . obey him, for the rest of her life, in sickness and in health, and all the other vicissitudes of marriage.

She glanced at his strong, rather solemn profile, and wondered if he was having second thoughts. Did he really love her? Did she love him? Sharon felt more confused than ever. Had she just let Janna convince her? She had mulled over and over in her mind every possible facet, and always she had come back to the same riveting fact—Bryce Townshend made her feel as no other man had ever done. But was it love?

She had not been the only one with doubts. Her mother had said carefully. 'Of course we're delighted, darling, but are you really quite sure? I mean . . . it's all a bit of a rush, isn't it? And you haven't known him all that long.'

Speaking to her parents by telephone, Sharon had bitten her lip and looked at the sapphire and diamond ring on her left hand for a long moment before she answered, 'I've known him a year.' But that wasn't strictly true. She hardly knew him at all.

At last the moment came when Bryce lifted her veil and pressed his lips briefly on hers. A wonderful warmth seemed to flow from him to her, and as she looked into his eyes and tried to read his expression, Bryce tucked her arm through his, and Janna moved forward to put her bouquet back in her hands. Then the photographer began to take pictures.

It was a beautiful day for a wedding, as just about everyone there had commented. Sharon looked up at the cloudless blue sky and wondered, 'Am I truly happy?'

Bryce pressed her hand, and she looked up at him. 'All right?' he whispered as the group began to reassemble around them for more photographs.

Sharon nodded.

'You look a bit pale,' he said solicitously.

'That's just your professional opinion!' she managed to tease. 'I'm fine.'

'No regrets?' He seemed almost anxious.

'Of course not!' Was she too vehement? She added, 'You?'

He laughed softly. 'I've got what I wanted.'

When the photography was over, Sharon and Bryce circulated amongst the guests, a colourful gathering in their summer dresses and hats. For the first time Sharon met friends of Bryce's, relatives, a whole new world of people that a month ago when he had proposed, she had scarcely known existed. She was nervous and a little shy, but everyone was friendly and wished them luck and happiness.

Bryce, she had been pleased to discover, got along well with her parents. Her father being a doctor helped, she supposed. She had been apprehensive that Bryce might be a little condescending towards him, a country GP, but after their first meeting, only yesterday, they had all gone out to dinner, she and her parents, and Bryce, and Sharon had felt ashamed of even thinking the thought. Her father and Bryce had got along famously.

Her mother's doubts had vanished too. Mrs Derwent had admitted that she liked Bryce immensely and said she was sure he would make an excellent husband. She had been a little concerned about their age difference, however.

'It's only twelve years,' Sharon had exclaimed. 'That's nothing!'

'No, I suppose it isn't,' Mrs Derwent had laughed. 'And you are twenty-five. It's not as though you're a teenager.' She added after a pause, 'I wonder why he left it so long to get married.'

'Do you mean you think he chose me as a last resort?' said Sharon lightly.

'No, dear, of course not,' amended her mother hastily. 'I didn't mean that at all. But he is attractive . . .'

'He lived with a woman for two years once,' Sharon eventually told her. 'It didn't work out. I think he must have fought shy of any close commitment since.'

A fleeting anxiety clouded her mother's face. 'I see. Yes, I imagine he would be the kind of man who would take a long time to get over that kind of thing. It probably left deep emotional scars.' She hugged her daughter. 'But I'm sure you'll be very happy, my darling. And I know you'll make him a wonderful wife.'

'I hope so,' Sharon said sincerely.

Once the wedding ceremony was over, Sharon felt a little less tense. Mingling with their guests, she became separated from Bryce eventually, but glimpsed him from time to time above the heads of other people, and each time she knew an eager impatience for them all to go home and leave her alone with him. Only then would she be sure that everything was going to be all right.

They were not going away on a honeymoon.

'We can get married right away,' Bryce had said, 'and have a honeymoon later, or we can wait a few months until it's convenient to do both.'

It was not possible, he had told her, to have a honeymoon straight away because that would mean cancelling operations, and he did not want to let down patients, some of whom had been waiting a long time, or pass them over to another surgeon.

It was also an awkward time because of imminent changes in the research team, of which Bryce was a part. A doctor from overseas was joining them, and Bryce was excited about his ideas, hoping that combined with his own research they would lead to progress towards more successful transplant techniques.

There were those of course who thought rushing into marriage was unwise, but Bryce was so eager to marry her at once that Sharon had let him persuade her.

'You can give up nursing now,' Bryce had said. 'You won't need to work any more, Sharon.'

She had insisted that she wanted to. 'At least for the time being,' she had said. 'I love my work, Bryce, and I don't want to give it up yet.'

He had smiled and kissed her. 'All right. It would be nursing's loss if you did.'

Sharon had been determined not to seek any special favours because she was marrying one of the surgeons, in a bit of a rush, so she had not asked for any extra time off, or any change in her rostered shifts, especially as they were short-staffed on Pinocchio anyway. The wedding was therefore arranged for a day when both Sharon and Bryce were off duty. Sharon was due back at the hospital the next morning, but she did not mind.

As Bryce had smilingly said, 'Just so long as you're not on nights for a while!'

'Sharon, dear, you look splendid!' It was the Gargoyle exclaiming, and Sharon could not help a wry smile. Effusive compliments from Sister Garland were treasures indeed.

'Lucky you,' remarked someone else. 'How did you manage to snare such a prize. Got any tips?'

There was laughter, more compliments, more good-natured ribbing as the champagne flowed. There were no speeches, but Sharon and Bryce cut a three-tiered cake, and afterwards Sharon tossed her bouquet to Janna.

'That should seal your fate,' she said laughing, and with a wink at Peter.

As they were not going anywhere, there was no need for the bride and groom to change into going-away clothes, and knowing this Sharon had chosen to be married in a short wedding dress with a shoulder-length veil fastened to her swept up hair with a circlet of tiny pearls, matching the pearl drop earrings given her by Bryce. They had been his mother's.

One of her aunts had been horrified. 'Pearls for sorrow!' she had warned ominously.

'Oh, Auntie, I'm not superstitious!' Sharon had laughed. 'I love pearls, and Bryce would be hurt if I didn't wear them.'

Sharon's dress of magnolia silk, was simple and elegant, with its close-fitting bodice and wide skirt with floating panels, and it was perfectly manageable for a wedding that required mingling with guests on a lawn. Her bouquet of creamy roses and pale green fern set it off exquisitely, complementing her auburn hair and honey-toned skin.

It had been Betsy Adamson, Bryce's housekeeper, who had paid Sharon the nicest compliment. Greeting her warmly when she arrived, Betsy had looked her over with her shrewd black eyes and said, 'I've always regarded Bryce as a son, and I hope you're going to let me think of you as a daughter.'

Sharon had kissed her. She had been a little afraid of Betsy when they had first met. Although obviously kindly, she still reminded Sharon of the strict nursing sister she must have been, and it was obvious she doted on Bryce. Sharon had been a little afraid she would be regarded as not good enough for him. Betsy's greeting had reassured her.

She was thinking of this as she and Bryce returned to the house after seeing some friends off. The shadows were lengthening as the sun dipped down towards the city skyline, and the wedding was drifting to a close as first one then another group of people wished them luck and left.

Bryce looked down at her. 'Nearly over.'

She smiled up at him. 'It went off quite well, I think.'

He nodded. His eyes were admiring. 'You make a

lovely bride.' He laughed. 'You should do it more often!'

'Oh, you!' she said, and squeezed his arm as they entered the hall.

Bryce glanced into the drawing room where several people were chatting. 'Someone I want to have a word with,' he murmured. 'Do you mind?'

'I must find Mum and Dad and see what they're doing,' Sharon said. 'See you outside in a minute.'

Bryce left her and Sharon continued on down the long hall. Passing a small antique table where wedding cards had been arranged she noticed that several had been knocked over and paused for a moment to set them up again. As she did so she heard voices coming from the small den-cum-television room just beside her. A couple of wedding guests were obviously taking the weight off their feet in there. She did not recognise the voices so they must be friends or relatives of Bryce's. Sharon had met too many people to be able to place them by their voices. In fact she probably would not even have noticed that anyone was there had not the sound of her own name, Bryce's, and another's, caught her attention. Automatically she tuned in.

'I don't know what to make of Bryce and Sharon to be quite candid,' declared a woman's voice. 'I mean, she's a pleasant girl, but is she really his type? I wonder if she knows Naomi's back.'

'I only heard yesterday,' replied her companion.

'*He* must know,' insisted the first speaker. 'Do you suppose that's the reason for the rushed wedding?'

There was an explosive, 'Oh! You don't mean . . .'

'You must admit it's odd,' said the first woman. 'A staff nurse, right out of the blue, just as though he'd stuck a pin in a list of names, or picked the one most likely to be seduced—although almost any one of that giddy romantic lot would have given their right arm to snare a good-looking senior surgeon, I'm sure!' There was a pause for laughter, then the first woman went on,

'It certainly looks as though he did it to spite Naomi.'

Her companion put in, 'Maybe he just thought it was time he got married. People do harp on it, you know.'

'Possible,' conceded the other woman, 'but it's my guess it's got more to do with Naomi than anything else. I'm glad I'm not in Sharon's shoes. I mean . . . you know how it was before . . .'

'Yes, but that was all over years ago.'

'He hasn't been in any hurry to marry until now, though. He always hoped she'd come back to him.'

'But she went off with another man.'

'She didn't marry him. What if she wants Bryce back now?'

'He might not want her back.'

The first woman laughed meaningfully. 'I wouldn't bank on that. They're going to be working together. I wonder how long it'll be before he can't keep his hands off her. If you ask me he's going to realise pretty soon that he's made a ghastly mistake.'

'Poor Sharon,' said her friend sympathetically.

'Yes, poor Sharon,' agreed the other woman. There were sounds of them moving about. 'Well, it's about time we said goodbye to them. Come on.'

Sharon who had stood frozen to the spot for the brief time the conversation had taken place, staring unseeingly at a wedding card in her hand, swiftly put it down and fled through the door at the end of the hall into the kitchen, hoping they had not emerged in time to see her and to realise she had been eavesdropping. The kitchen was temporarily empty. Sharon sank onto a chair and put her head in her hands. A few moments later, Bryce found her there. Sharon drew back as though stung at his tentative touch.

'Sharon . . . are you all right?' He was all concern, and looking up at him, she knew suddenly, without any shadow of doubt, that she loved him. Why there had been any uncertainty before was a mystery. She looked into his face and felt for the first time in her life, the terrible blinding hurt of jealousy.

'You're not well . . .' He squatted beside her chair, holding both her hands in his, then he felt her brow, his own creasing anxiously. 'The excitement . . . it's been too much for you.'

Sharon found her voice. 'No, really, Bryce, I'm quite all right. I just wanted to sit down for a minute, that's all. I've been standing for a long time.'

He looked dubious. 'Stop pretending. Nurses are used to being on their feet all day.'

One of the caterers' assistants came in and Sharon abruptly stood up. 'Oh, do stop fussing, Bryce,' she said edgily. 'I'm perfectly all right.'

He looked a little put out at her terse tone, but he did not pursue it, and when she swept out of the kitchen, he followed in silence. It was almost as though they'd had a tiff, Sharon thought, her throat constricting as she pinned back on the bright smile, the radiant-bride look everyone expected of her, and said goodbye to the remaining guests. Although she smiled and thanked everyone, their words of congratulation and good wishes barely registered. In her mind she heard only one refrain over and over, 'Naomi's back . . . how long before he can't keep his hands off her . . . ghastly mistake . . . poor Sharon . . . poor Sharon . . .'

Her parents and some of Bryce's close relatives were amongst the last to leave. Sharon's mother and father were staying at a hotel overnight and driving home to Winnabri tomorrow. Sharon felt tears springing into her eyes as her mother hugged her and said, moist-eyed herself, 'I hope you'll be very happy, darling. It was a beautiful wedding, and Bryce is a lovely man.'

Her father clasped her emotionally and said, 'I know Bryce will take good care of you.'

'You can rely on that,' murmured Bryce at her side.

At last only Betsy was left, and the girls from the caterers who were clearing up. Sharon could see that Betsy was itching to lend a hand but Bryce had insisted she do nothing. She in her turn had insisted on going to stay with her sister for a couple of days.

'You'll want to be quite alone,' she had said emphatically, 'on your wedding night.'

After seeing her off in a taxi, Sharon and Bryce walked slowly back into the house. Bryce's arm was around Sharon and he squeezed her shoulders. 'Well, Mrs Townshend, feeling better now?' There was still anxiety in his eyes.

'Yes, I'm all right.' Her voice had an edge to it she could not help.

As they went into the drawing room where two of the caterers' assistants were clearing away glasses and plates and empty champagne bottles, Bryce said, 'We might as well change now, I suppose. Feels a bit silly all togged up like this when it's over, doesn't it?'

One of the girls from the caterers approached them, carrying an ice-bucket. 'Here's a bottle of champagne, Dr Townshend,' she said smiling, 'Why don't you both sit down and have a nice quiet relaxing drink. We've just about finished.'

Bryce glanced at Sharon. 'Shall we? We both need to wind down a bit, I'm sure. Let's drink a toast to ourselves!'

Sharon nodded. She had hardly drunk any champagne during the afternoon and the thought of the cool sparkling wine was tempting. She was not sure that she wanted to go upstairs yet. She had the feeling she'd always had at examination times, that she wanted to run away as far as possible and not go through with it. But she had to now. She was married to Bryce, for better or worse . . .

She sank wearily onto the sofa, kicking off her shoes, and putting her feet up while Bryce opened the champagne. She removed her veil and laid it across the arm of the sofa. She twisted the two rings—the sapphire engagement ring and the plain gold wedding band, bemusedly. It hardly seemed possible that she was Mrs Bryce Townshend. Less than three months ago the idea would have seemed utterly ridiculous.

Bryce handed her a glass of champagne, gently moved her legs aside so that he could sit beside her, and touched his glass to hers. His eyes were smiling tentatively. He seemed a little apprehensive of her.

'To . . . us,' he murmured.

Sharon managed a wan smile as their glasses clinked.

'Did I tell you how beautiful you look today?' Bryce said softly. He tilted her chin with a forefinger to look more closely into her face. 'Like an angel. When the breeze blew the panels of your dress around it was as though you had wings.' He looked at her earnestly. 'You won't ever fly away from me, will you?' His lips touched hers, and instantly kindled the flames of desire.

There was an odd look in his eyes, almost as though he doubted her. But surely it was he who might fly away from her, she thought, miserably. She sipped her champagne and tried to put such thoughts out of her mind. They chatted idly about the wedding, discussing the guests, her parents, and interspersing their conversation with small but meaningful silences. Sharon almost blurted out several times what she had overheard, but always bit the words back.

At last Bryce stretched and yawned and then turned to her. She could barely see his face now in the fading light. It had grown suddenly quite dark in the room whose windows were heavily overshadowed by the jacaranda in the front garden.

'Well, that's the end of the champagne,' Bryce said. 'Shall we go up now?'

He stood up, and remained looking down at her for a moment or two. Then he bent and effortlessly plucked her from the couch and began to carry her upstairs.

'Bryce . . . you fool!' Sharon protested, feeling suddenly light-headed after the champagne.

He laughed. 'This counts as carrying you over the threshold!'

He strode up the stairs with ease, her weight seemingly nothing to him. He kicked open the door of the big bedroom and bore her in, kicking the door closed behind him. The room was dim because the curtains were already drawn. Bryce laid Sharon laughing and protesting on the bed.

'My shoes . . . I left my shoes . . .' she giggled helplessly. When she attempted to get up, he pinned her down with his body and kissed her long and hungrily.

Sharon melted into his arms willingly, determined to forget what she had overheard. That was just gossip. She must not let gossip spoil her wedding night. When Bryce had had enough of kissing her, he clasped her hands and drew her to her feet. Her hair was already disarrayed, and he now removed the combs that had held it in place and let the lustrous auburn tresses fall about her shoulders. He tossed the combs across the room, not taking his eyes from her face for a moment. Then he lifted one side of her hair and slid his fingers around the back of her neck.

Slowly and methodically he began to remove her wedding gown, kissing her and smiling at her while she stood as though mesmerised. His hands lingered caressingly on her smooth shoulders as he brushed the straps of her slip aside and he drew her briefly against him, kissing the hollows of her neck, and the breathlessly rising and falling swell of her breasts. He did not hurry, as though what he was doing was something he wanted to prolong and savour. When at last she stood naked before him he held her a little way from him, devouring her for a moment with his eyes, and then sweeping the covers from the bed, he picked her up in one swift movement and laid her on the cool undersheet, drawing the top one over her.

Sharon lay tense and trembling as he began to undress, barely able to see him now in the deepening gloom. The house was absolutely still and silent. From what seemed a very long way off came the murmur of traffic, but the louder sound crashed through the stillness, startling her into instantly sitting bolt upright.

She heard Bryce say, 'Damn!' as the telephone continued to shrill insistently on the bedside table.

His hand reached for it automatically, then hovered for a split second of indecision and Sharon knew he was debating whether to answer or not. Eventually he picked up the receiver.

'Townshend.' His voice was curt.

Sharon knew instinctively that it was the hospital, and Bryce's next words confirmed it.

'Right, I'll be there as soon as I can. No . . . you did the right thing. I said call me.' He glanced at Sharon. 'She won't run away!'

The receiver fell back onto the rest and he let out a long breath as he switched on the bedside lamp. It filled the room with a mellow light that at first was dazzling. His expression was grim.

Sharon said, 'The hospital?'

'Yes. An emergency I'm afraid. I half expected it but I was hoping not today.' He added briskly, 'A complication in an artery by-pass I performed two days ago. Sheldon didn't want to ring me in the circumstances but he knew I had insisted they must if necessary.' He paused a moment then added soberly, 'The patient is only forty-nine.' He looked steadily at Sharon, then reached for her hand and squeezed it. 'Sorry . . .'

Sharon felt somehow foolish, and embarrassed sitting up in the bed holding the sheet up to her chin watching as he wrenched a pair of ordinary trousers and a shirt from the wardrobe and hastily scrambled into them. There ought to be something she could do to help, she thought helplessly.

He bent and kissed her briefly, and a moment later he was gone, leaving her with only the breath of his fleeting kiss and the hope that the patient might not be as bad as Dr Sheldon feared and that Bryce would be back soon.

She heard the front door slam and the car drive away. For a long time she remained where she was, staring at the blue velvet jacket and trousers, the white wedding shirt, the pale blue tie, all lying in a crumpled heap on the floor beside her own filmy wedding gown. It was no use feeling disappointed. Life from now on was often going to be like this. With Bryce a patient's life would always come before his own pleasures. And she wouldn't have it any other way.

Finally she got up, put on a dressing gown, tidied their wedding clothes away and went downstairs to the kitchen to make some coffee. The remains of the wedding cake were on the table, under a cover. Sharon nibbled a few crumbs of the thick royal icing and marzipan, and smiled ruefully at the tiny doll bride and groom—they looked so cute . . .

She sighed, and realising suddenly that her earlobes ached because she was still wearing her pearl drop earrings, unclipped them and laid them on the table. Unbidden, her aunt's superstitious warning came back, but she quickly chased it away. It was silly to be superstitious.

At midnight she went wearily up to bed. There was no sign of Bryce, no call from the hospital to tell her what was happening. She felt it would be unreasonable to ring and ask. She slept fitfully, starting awake at every small sound, at every car that turned into the street, in case it was Bryce returning. But at dawn she was still alone.

CHAPTER FIVE

BRYCE came back just as Sharon was hurriedly downing coffee and a slice of toast. He came straight into the kitchen and she was shocked at his appearance. Haggard was the only word for it.

'Bryce . . .' Instinctively she went to him and touched his arm. He looked at her with glazed eyes and slumped into a chair. 'Coffee?' She withdrew and poured a cup for him, sensing that he did not want any personal contact.

'Thanks . . .' He looked at her, almost as though she was a stranger. 'The patient died,' he said simply.

'Oh.' There were no words of consolation that would help, she knew.

He ran his fingers agitatedly through his hair. 'There's got to be a way . . .'

'A way for what?' she asked gently.

He looked at her, his eyes blazing suddenly with a fierce determination.

'Giving people new hearts that won't wear out before they do.'

'You mean transplants that work—permanently?'

'Exactly. The heart of the man who died this morning was one that was really beyond repair. He was only forty-nine, Sharon.' He reached for her hand and clasped it tightly, twining his fingers with hers, but said nothing more.

She withdrew her hand. 'I'll have to go, Bryce. I'm on duty at eight.'

He looked vaguely at her. 'Yes . . . of course . . . I lost all sense of time I'm afraid. You go, I'll fix myself some breakfast.'

Sharon looked at him, this man who was her husband—well, according to her marriage certificate he was, but was he? Would theirs ever be the kind of marriage she had dreamed of?

He caught her hand again as she moved past his chair and pulled her unresisting into his arms and buried his face against her breast.

'Sorry about last night,' he muttered.

'No need to be,' she said, and stroked his hair soothingly. 'In our kind of job we know we have to put up with interruptions.'

'We should have organised it better, a proper honeymoon right away,' he said.

'All in good time.'

He raised his head and gave her a rueful smile. 'Tonight I shall take the phone off the hook!'

She laughed softly. 'You know you won't.'

'Kiss me.'

Sharon bent her head and touched his lips with hers. He tried to turn it into passion but although his nearness fanned her own desires almost unbearably, she wrested herself reluctantly away from him. 'I'll be late, Bryce, and you know what Sister Garland is.'

'The Gargoyle!' He chuckled, and Sharon involuntarily flinched. So he knew what the nurses called her. She wondered if Sister Garland herself knew.

Bryce said, 'She'll understand. After all, you were married only yesterday.'

'Sister Garland does not understand anything personal that interferes with hospital duty,' said Sharon. 'Even weddings. She didn't approve of us getting married now. She said we ought to wait until we could both take leave.'

'She would! She thinks everybody is as cold a fish as she is!'

'You should feel sorry for her,' Sharon rebuked.

He laughed wickedly. 'I am! I'd be even sorrier for anyone she married, though. I bet he'd have to make an application in triplicate and give a week's notice to share her bed!'

Sharon was glad to see the sombre mood lifting a little, and the sense of humour that in the past few weeks she had discovered did lurk beneath the austere front he normally presented asserting itself, despite the rigours of the night. She longed to spend the day with him and it took a great effort of will to break away from him and run upstairs to brush her teeth, but as she had not officially asked for time off it would be irresponsible of her to take it now. Besides, the staffing situation at South City was almost crucial at the moment.

Bryce followed her a few minutes later. 'I'll drive you,' he said, standing in the bathroom doorway as she fixed the combs into her swept-up and neatly coiled hair.

Sharon shook her head. 'You'll do no such thing. You'll go straight to bed and get some sleep. You're worn out.'

'I don't like you riding to work,' he said.

They had argued about this already because he considered it was too dangerous.

Sharon put her foot down. 'I most certainly shall. By the time I walk down to the tram stop and change trams in town, I'll be hours late. Don't be unreasonable, Bryce. I'm a very experienced cyclist, and I can cope with traffic.'

'It's much further to the hospital from here,' he objected, 'and you have to go through the city.'

'Don't fuss,' she retorted, 'I'm already late.'

He grabbed her hand and kissed her again as she swept past him.

Pedalling easily along with the light early-morning traffic, Sharon reflected on her wedding day and night. It all seemed so unreal, somehow, and it was only the fact that she was going to work by a different route that convinced her it had all happened. She reached the hospital only a few minutes late, and although Sister

Garland pursed her lips in disapproval she did not reprimand her.

Sister said archly, 'I suppose you're bound to be somewhat jaded after yesterday. Perhaps you should have swapped shifts with someone after all.'

Sharon answered with a smile, 'I feel fine, actually, Sister. Not a bit tired. It was much less strain having the wedding at home.'

Sister Garland looked her over. 'What a pity Dr Townshend had to spend most of the night at the hospital.' She thrust a sheaf of forms at Sharon and went on briskly, 'I'd like you to take these prescriptions down to the Dispensary, if you don't mind, Nurse Der . . . Townshend.'

Sharon was half inclined to refuse since running messages was a job for the junior and student nurses, but she had the feeling that Sister Garland wanted to keep her in her place, to show her that she was not to get any high and mighty ideas because of her new situation as Dr Townshend's wife. Sharon had no intention of using that as a lever to gain any favours for herself, so she took the prescriptions without a murmur.

The morning passed swiftly. Today most of the children wanted to hear about the wedding and Sharon was obliged to describe the ceremony and her dress and the bridesmaid's dress, over and over. There was, as usual, a great deal of interest in the food, and Sharon had to promise to show them the photographs of the wedding just as soon as they were ready.

It was lunchtime before Sharon realised it, and it was only after the meal was over that things quietened down for a while. Most of the children settled down for a rest in the afternoon. Sharon heaved a small sigh of relief as she paused to look back down the ward. The mix was the usual one. There were always some boisterous children, usually one or two quiet and unobtrusive ones. There were always those who clamoured for all her attention, and those who waited patiently for their turn. Sometimes they could be very exasperating, despite their illnesses, but she could not help loving them all. There was something so uncomplicated about children. They were so tough and yet so vulnerable.

She looked across the ward at one of the recent admissions, Natalie, a frail child suffering from a congenital hip deformity requiring a pelvic osteotomy, and reminded herself to buy a get-well card. Natalie was the only child in the ward who didn't have any. She didn't have daily visitors either. Her parents were country people who could not get down to Melbourne often. Sharon reminded herself to try and spend more time with Natalie, especially when the ward was full of visitors.

As she turned to go into the duty room to start writing up her reports while the ward was quiet, two people came through the double doors beyond Sister's office.

One of the other nurses, coming up behind Sharon, said, 'Hello, I wonder what Aunt Sally wants. And who's the film star?'

Aunt Sally was the Director of Nursing's own nickname for herself, given one day when crisis had followed crisis and she had declared roundly, 'I get everything thrown at me in this hospital! I'm just an Aunt Sally!' She was in fact a very competent and very well liked DN, exceedingly conscientious about her overall responsibility for the actions of her staff.

Sharon glanced at the approaching pair and saw why Jean Watkins had said film star. The woman with the DN was strikingly beautiful, with rivetting deep blue eyes, carefully arched brows, and a helmet of sleek black hair, shiny and smooth as satin, clinging around her heart-shaped face. Her full red lips were sensuous but, Sharon thought, hard, suggesting she would seldom tolerate opposition to her will. She moved with a slinky grace that was accentuated rather than disguised by the loose-fitting blue dress she wore. She was about thirty, Sharon guessed, and probably even more attractive now in maturity than she had been as a girl. She wondered who she was. Aunt Sally seemed to be treating her rather like a Royal visitor.

The DN looked into Sister's office, saw that she was not there, and approached Sharon. 'Sister's at lunch, I suppose?'

'Yes. Can I help at all?' Sharon offered.

The DN beamed at her. 'I expect you can, Nurse Derwent . . .' At once she corrected herself with a smile. 'Forgive me . . . Nurse Townshend now isn't it?' She gave a small apologetic laugh and turned to the woman visitor. 'Nurse Townshend was married yesterday. To our Dr Bryce Townshend. I wonder if he was here in your time? The poor things haven't even had a honeymoon. I think it's very noble of Sharon to come to work this morning, don't you? And Dr Townshend was here most of the night for an emergency. They really ought to have arranged things better.' She laughed sympathetically.

Her sympathy was not mirrored in the glamorous visitor's face, however. Her finely boned features changed almost imperceptibly, but Sharon noticed a sudden flickering of her long dark lashes, and the faint quiver at the corners of her mouth that suggested she was taken aback, if not deeply shocked by something. Before Sharon could wonder why, Aunt Sally was saying:

'This is Dr Naomi Forrest. She has recently returned from America . . . having a little holiday in Tahiti on the way . . . and she is joining our cardiology unit. She practised here before she went abroad some years ago, before my time.' She took a breath and went on in her inimitably garrulous way, 'So things won't be entirely unfamiliar to her, although she's keen to reorient herself with all sections of the hospital. We are very lucky to have her back, as I expect your husband has told you, because her experience in the United States is bound to be invaluable in the work we are doing here. I think we can look forward to great strides in cardiology at South City General now we have such a brilliant team. With Dr Townshend and Dr Forrest working together, who knows what will happen.'

Sharon listened with a dull, sick feeling deep inside her. So this was Naomi, the woman who had lived with Bryce and who had walked out on him. He must know Naomi was rejoining the team, but he had not told her. He had only told her about a doctor from England. Had he really married her to spite Naomi, as those wedding guests she had overheard had suggested? Indeed, who knew what might happen now.

'How do you do?' Sharon said politely, her voice quite level although she was quaking inside.

Dr Forrest encompassed her with one swift appraising glance. Her composure was intact, and if her glance was a trifle condescending, her voice was friendly, and gave nothing away.

'How do you do?' she replied, adding, 'Yes, I remember Dr Townshend.' To Sharon she said in cool tones. 'Congratulations.'

The DN smilingly plunged on. 'He's a dark horse, our Dr Townshend. Just when we all thought he was a confirmed bachelor, he marries Sharon.' She beamed at Sharon. 'I hear you made a lovely couple, and you were quite stunning as a bride.' Then abruptly she changed tack. 'I'd like to leave Dr Forrest with you for a few minutes, if I may. I have someone waiting to be interviewed.' She glanced at Naomi. 'It won't take long. I shall be through by the time you've seen over the ward, and then perhaps you would care to come back to my office.'

'Very well . . . thank you,' agreed Naomi Forrest with a rather forced smile.

When the DN had gone, and Sharon and Naomi were alone, Sharon realised that she was shaking.

Naomi now looked her over, more incisively this time, and with a definitely superior air. 'How long have you

been nursing here?' she inquired in a soft voice which
Sharon felt held dangerous undertones.

'Just over a year,' she answered.

The girl studied her intently. 'You know of course that
Bryce and I . . .'

'Yes,' Sharon said at once. 'He told me.' She was
taken aback by Naomi's blunt approach.

Naomi interlaced her fingers and glanced down at
them demurely.

'Forgive me for mentioning it,' she said. There was a
suggestion of American intonation in her well-
modulated voice. She looked up apologetically. 'I
thought we had better not begin with secrets, especially
as I shall be working alongside Bryce.'

'I'm sorry it didn't work out for you,' murmured
Sharon, feeling more ill at ease than she had ever done in
her life.

A light lilting laugh escaped the other woman's lips.
'We . . . well I was too young . . . too impulsive.' Her
face closed up abruptly as she added, 'I guess we've both
matured a good deal.'

Her words had a cut and thrust that made Sharon
squirm. The remarks were tossed off innocently and
offhandedly enough, but Sharon was aware of an underlying threat. Naomi Forrest, she felt instinctively, was
still in love with Bryce. Perhaps it was the very reason
why she had come back. The fact that he was married
had certainly shocked her. Either no-one had told her
out of tact, or there had not been time to. She had been
on holiday in Tahiti before returning to Melbourne
which might account for her ignorance.

'I have to admit,' Naomi said next, 'that I was quite
flabbergasted a few moments ago when the DN told me
Bryce was married.' She laughed nonchalantly. 'Uncle
Les never mentioned it.' At Sharon's expression she
explained. 'My godfather, Sir Leslie Ponting. No doubt
you've heard of him.'

Sharon had certainly heard of Sir Leslie Ponting, an

eminent medical scientist, now retired, whom Bryce respected almost devoutly. What she had not known was that he was Naomi's godfather.

Naomi, with an all-encompassing look that suggested incredulity, remarked, 'I suppose you must have something, my dear!'

She's upset, thought Sharon, but so am I. And I'm frightened too.

'You'll have to ask Bryce about that, Dr-Forrest,' Sharon countered with a thin smile. 'And now, would you like to see the ward? I have quite a lot to do . . .'

The glamorous doctor accepted the rebuff well, with just a suggestion of raised eyebrows and a mildly challenging look in her eyes. 'Very well,' she said.

Sharon escorted her around the ward, stopping to speak to one or two of the children who were not asleep, and to explain their particular problems to the newcomer. She managed to keep a clam exterior while all the time her emotions were churning with a sickening fear. Naomi was cool and direct, very professional in the way she asked penetrating clinical questions, which Sharon sometimes had difficulty in answering since she was not a doctor herself. Although Naomi smiled constantly, paid small compliments, and seemed interested, Sharon had the feeling that she was deliberately trying to make her feel inferior. The rub was that she was succeeding.

As they walked back towards the duty room Naomi talked about her time in America and recent advances in cardiology, dropping names blithely—a whole host of names Sharon had never heard of—and giving Sharon darting glances and smiles that said she knew it was all above a mere nurse's head, and was meant to be.

Sharon, only half-listening, was relieved when she saw Sister Garland approaching. Now she would be able to get rid of her visitor. Then, to her surprise, she realised that behind the Gargoyle was Bryce. Sharon drew a sharp breath. She had not expected him to come in again today. His face, when he saw Naomi, who had turned away for a moment to read a notice on the wall and was apparently unaware of him, seemed to close right up, and Sharon had the feeling that although he must have known of her return, this was the first time he had encountered her.

'Naomi . . .' His voice sounded hoarse, and his eyes were only for the dark-haired doctor, Sharon noticed with a sinking heart. He was drinking her in like a man who had been dying of thirst. He seemed unaware that Sharon was even there.

Dr Forrest turned round, her eyes widening, not in surprise, but instantaneous pleasure as she realised who had spoken. Her lips parted slowly in the kind of smile only someone who has been intimate with the other person can give.

'Why, Bryce,' she said nonchalantly, 'I hadn't expected to bump into you today. I understood you were on all night . . . and I believe you got married yesterday!' She made it sound as though it were some kind of joke.

'I wasn't expecting to see you so soon,' he said, his voice perfectly controlled, without the slightest crack in it to betray his feelings. He was standing close to her, looking down at her petite figure while Sharon wished desperately she knew what was in his mind at that moment.

Naomi held out her hand. Her laughter was low and, Sharon thought, sexy. 'You know me, Bryce. I couldn't wait to get back to work, so I cut my holiday short.'

Bryce said, rather brusquely, 'I thought you'd found your niche in the States.'

Naomi inclined her head slightly and regarded him with a hint of coquettishness. 'I thought so too . . . once . . . but there were things back here in Australia that I always longed for.'

Her eyes devoured him and her words, Sharon felt certain, were as meaningful to Bryce as they were to her.

Bryce kept her hand just a little too long—or was she being silly? Sharon thought—and then seemed to release it reluctantly. He thrust his hands into the pockets of his white coat.

Sister Garland, feeling no doubt rather left out, interposed. 'I don't think our visitor and I have met.'

'I'm sorry, Sister,' Sharon began, but Bryce stepped in and made the introduction.

Naomi smiled rather patronisingly at the Gargoyle, then said pleasantly enough, 'It was kind of Nurse Townshend to show me round the ward. But I really mustn't take up any more of your time. The DN told me how short-staffed the hospital is at the moment.' She turned to Bryce with a winning smile. 'The DN went off to conduct an interview, so if she's still engaged, you can amuse me for a little while, I hope.' She turned a rather insincere smile on Sharon. 'Thank you for a most interesting tour, Nurse.'

Bryce made no protest and the two of them melted away, leaving Sharon clenching her fists in an effort to stop the ugly wave of jealousy that was scorching through her. Naomi had waltzed off with Bryce as though he still belonged to her, and he had gone as meekly as though he did. He had evidently forgotten whatever it was he had come down to Pinocchio for.

Sister Garland eyed Sharon sharply. 'Attractive woman,' she observed.

'Very,' agreed Sharon. 'Clever too, I gather.'

Sister Garland laughed a little unkindly. 'You'll have to watch out for that husband of yours. She looks predatory to me.' There was a certain amount of veiled malice in her remark, but Sharon did not think she knew about Bryce and Naomi once living together. It must have been before her time too. But some people at South City General were bound to remember, she thought miserably, and they would be sure to gossip about it now that Naomi was back.

It seemed the longest shift Sharon had ever worked

that day. It was impossible to keep her mind away from thoughts of Bryce and Naomi for more than a few minutes, and she had never been more glad in her life than when it was time to hand over to the next shift. She felt utterly weary, but knew it was emotional rather than physical tiredness that had drained her energy and her spirit. On her way to the cloakroom, she met Janna in a corridor.

'Sharon . . . how's everything?' Janna looked her over as though expecting to find some momentous change in her, then she said, 'Pardon me for saying so, but you look whacked!' She giggled. 'Serves you right for getting married one day and going back to work the next. I told you people need honeymoons.'

Sharon raised a smile. 'We're going to have one, all in good time, don't worry.' Would they, she suddenly thought, or was this just a dream and one day soon she would suffer a rude awakening?

'It was a beautiful wedding,' said Janna dreamily. 'You looked absolutely divine, Sharon, and Bryce is really the most gorgeous hunk of man—you lucky girl. He was so . . . so human yesterday. It must be your doing. I swear every single woman there was envious as hell of you, and probably most of the married ones were as well!'

'I think most people were still just surprised,' said Sharon.

'I'll say they were! You really rocked 'em, Sharon, snaring Bryce.' She lowered her voice, 'And don't worry about what some people say . . .'

Sharon started. 'What are they saying?'

Janna shrugged. 'You know . . . there's bound to be a certain amount of pique because he's married a staff nurse.'

'A bit beneath him you mean?'

'Well, you said it. But what matters is that Bryce doesn't think so. He knows why he married you.'

'Yes,' murmured Sharon, bleakly, 'I guess he does.'

Janna said confidentially, 'Actually, I think your get-ting married has given Peter ideas at last. He started talking about "us" and "our house" last night, which is promising.' She paused. 'Heavens, I nearly forgot. I knew there was something I meant to ask you. I'm on the committee organising the annual fund-raising campaign. Will you help?'

'What doing?' Sharon asked cautiously.

'Nothing much. We need a few more volunteers for the bed marathon . . . some to push, some to ride on hospital beds all the way to the City Square. It was a great success last year. Do you want to push, or be a patient and wave a bedpan to collect donations?'

Sharon was a bit doubtful. 'I don't know . . .'

'Come on,' urged Janna, 'don't start getting all uppity just because you're a senior surgeon's wife now.'

'Janna, I'm not getting all uppity . . .' Sharon was dismayed.

Janna grinned. 'I know you're not! Only joking. So I can put you down as a pusher then? You can also shake a collection box in the Square.' She glanced at the clock above them on the wall. 'Help . . . I've got masses to do before I knock off. See you later. Give me a ring sometime and come over for a natter.'

As Sharon wheeled her bicycle out and mounted it, she glanced across at the parking area. Bryce's car was still there. What was he doing? she wondered. Still with Naomi Forrest?

'Oh, stop it,' she scolded herself as she braked sav-agely near the hospital gates, almost colliding with an ambulance leaving. 'Jealousy is destructive.'

It seemed strange to be riding home to East Mel-bourne instead of back to the flat she had shared with Janna. It seemed even stranger letting herself into the strange house. This morning she had been in a rush and had not had time to dwell on the unfamiliarity of it all. Now, as she put her key in the lock, the full impact of her changed life suddenly began to overwhelm her. She was

Mrs Bryce Townshend, wife of a highly respected surgeon, mistress of this beautiful house and its contents. She gazed around her, drinking it all in, still unable to believe that this was where she belonged, still feeling uncomfortable and a little out of place. And unbidden came the thought that Naomi would never have felt like that.

She wandered into the kitchen. Only the remains of the cake still on the table recalled yesterday's wedding. Betsy Adamson would not be back until later on this evening, but there was no need for Sharon to do any real cooking as the housekeeper had left a casserole in the refrigerator for tonight's dinner. Sharon took it out and switched the oven on.

It was seven o'clock when she heard Bryce's key in the door. She raced out of the den where she was watching the news on television, and turned the oven up high. Then she ran down the hall to greet him, feeling foolishly apprehensive and almost as nervous as she had been on their first date.

'You're home . . .' she stammered, stopping abruptly in front of him. 'Dinner's nearly ready.'

He regarded her for a moment, as though surprised to find this stranger in the house, almost as though, she thought, he had forgotten she would be there. Then he gathered her firmly into his arms and kissed her long and thoroughly. She felt her strangeness melting away.

'Sharon,' he said at last, looking into her eyes. 'You don't know how good it is to find you here when I come home.'

'I won't always be,' she reminded him. 'Shifts, you know.'

'We'll have to pull a few strings.'

She shook her head. 'It wouldn't look good.'

'No, perhaps not. Mmm, that's a delicious aroma.'

'All due to Betsy, I'm afraid,' she confessed. 'But as soon as I get properly organised, I'll show you I can cook!'

'Betsy's coming back tonight, isn't she?' he remarked.

'Yes.' Sharon smiled. 'I don't think she believes I could look after you properly if she left you for too long.'

He chuckled. 'I'm afraid she has spoiled me.' His eyes met hers. 'But I'm sure you would look after me very well.' With a change of tone he added, 'You don't mind Betsy remaining here?'

'Of course not! She's a dear. But I'm not used to having things done for me. It makes me feel lazy.'

He chuckled again. 'You'll get used to it.' His arm slipped about her waist as they went through to the kitchen. While she attended to the meal, he poured them both a drink and perched on a stool at the break-fast-bar watching her as she dashed from stove to sink to work top. Whenever she caught his eye, it was speculative and she wondered what he was thinking. Was he remembering when Naomi had flitted about his kitchen—Betsy hadn't been here then—comparing the two of them. Somehow she couldn't imagine Naomi being fond of domestic chores, but Bryce might not have been able to afford a housekeeper then. She did not ask.

Bryce did not mention Dr Forrest, and Sharon resisted the urge to ask him about her, although she very much wanted to. She did not want him to guess that she was jealous. And besides, they had agreed not to talk shop at home—at least not all the time. Sharon was aware that where Bryce's work was concerned, she would not be able to contribute much anyway.

It came as a surprise, therefore, when, over coffee, he suddenly broached the subject of Naomi himself.

'Naomi said what a delightful girl you are.' He looked across at her, smiling fondly.

Sharon flushed slightly. 'Did she?' She was more flattered that Bryce had repeated it, than that Naomi had said it. She couldn't believe the woman had been sincere.

He chuckled. 'I think she was rather taken aback to find that I was married. Evidently Sir Leslie . . . that's

Sir Leslie Ponting, her godfather, the medical scientist I've mentioned . . . didn't mention it. I thought he would have done.'

'I imagine he was trying to be tactful,' said Sharon, adding, 'Perhaps she was hoping you were not.'

His eyes narrowed fractionally. 'Mmm. I suppose it might have given her some satisfaction to have found that no-one else would have what she had cast off.'

'Or that you couldn't find anyone to compare with her.' Sharon wished she could erase the edge from her tone.

Bryce reached for her hand. 'Why make comparisons? An odious thing to do, I've always believed. You are you, Naomi is Naomi. You are two vastly different people . . . vastly different.'

'I imagine we are,' Sharon commented dryly, adding straight away, while she had the courage, 'You didn't tell me she was coming back to South City General. You only mentioned that a doctor from England was joining the team.'

His eyes narrowed slightly and he had the grace to look a little uncomfortable. 'I'm sorry, I should have mentioned it, but I was afraid it might upset you.' His eyes searched her face. 'Sharon, you're not upset are you? You know that was all over years ago. I'm married to you now. Naomi is no more than a colleague.'

Sharon wished she had not spoken. He had made her feel like a prying wife. She wanted to believe what he said was true, but knew he would never admit to her that he had married her to spite Naomi. And even if he hadn't, working with Naomi again might show him what a mistake he had made. 'How long before he can't keep his hands off her?' The horrible words still echoed in her mind.

She said, 'I suppose you're going to be very busy.'

He smiled, and seemed to forget their previous exchange. 'For a few months, yes, and it's going to be exciting, I hope! Dr Chris Hargreaves arrives from

London in a day or two. He's been studying transplants for some years and has some advanced ideas. I was skimming through one of his most recent papers only today and he reckons . . .' He stopped abruptly. 'But I mustn't start getting technical. It'd be all double dutch to you.' He raised her hand to his lips.

Sharon drew her hand away. 'I'm not a complete idiot you know! I might understand more than you think. I do read medical journals too! Just because I'm only a staff nurse . . .'

'Sharon . . . don't be silly . . . I wasn't denigrating you! We agreed not to talk shop, remember? There's no need to be so touchy.' His annoyance showed even though he was obviously trying to conceal it. Sharon wished she had not spoken so tetchily.

'I'm not touchy,' she said shortly.

He stretched out an arm, encircled her shoulders and drew her against him. She could not resist him and snuggled willingly into his embrace. When he raised his lips from hers he looked at her with mounting desire. 'Come on, let's go to bed.'

'The dishes . . .' she muttered.

'Hang the dishes!' He was on his feet and laughingly scooped her up in his arms. 'Now, let's start again from the beginning, Mrs Townshend, or have you forgotten already that you promised to obey?'

'Bryce . . . you idiot!' she exclaimed as he carried her upstairs again.

'Betsy will be very suspicious if she finds us still gossiping in the drawing room when she comes home,' he said, laughing. 'She'll think we've had a tiff!'

A few moments later, lying beside her, running tender tantalising fingers over her skin, teasing her with gentle caresses, fanning her need for him into a consuming fire, he murmured, 'You really do have a beautiful body.'

His lips touched hers, lightly, then with firmness and precision urged hers apart, moulding their mouths together in a violent seeking that sent the first waves of ecstasy coursing through her. Her fingers clutched his hair, drew him down as hard as she could, eager for the consummation of their love, to know that he really loved her.

But suddenly, without warning, thoughts of Naomi filled her mind. She thought of Bryce making love to Naomi. That was no fantasy. She knew that he had. He had lived with her. He knew her intimately. His hands had caressed her, his lips had tasted her. He had loved Naomi as he was loving her now . . . in this very bed . . . and Naomi's body was so much more beautiful than hers . . . Naomi still wanted Bryce, of that Sharon was certain, but did he still love her?

A wave of revulsion swept over her that was like the nausea of illness. She could not bear his touch, she could not bear to think of those same hands touching Naomi, those lips kissing the other woman, and probably still wanting to. 'How long can he keep his hands off her?' The mocking words rang in her ears. How long? It had been naive of her to imagine that love-making would provide proof of love.

Sharon dragged herself abruptly from his embrace, all her response withering in an instant, her body feeling as chilled as though she stood under a cold shower.

'Sharon . . . what's the matter?' Bryce's voice, husky with desire, was tinged with anxiety.

'Nothing . . .' Her own voice was a croak. How could she explain her feeling of humiliation?

'Nothing?' he demanded impatiently.

'I . . . I can't . . .' she stammered inadequately.

His hand touched her, stroking gently. 'Sharon . . .' he coaxed.

'No . . .' she whimpered.

He turned her towards him, tenderly. 'Don't be silly, I won't hurt you . . .'

She recoiled as though stung. 'No . . . leave me alone . . .' Tears were starting behind her eyes. She leapt out of bed, snatched up her dressing gown and flinging it on ran to the bathroom and closed the door.

In a moment he was outside the door, sounding very annoyed now. 'Sharon, what is this? What the hell's the matter with you?'

'Nothing.'

'Look, if you say that again . . .'

'Go away . . .' She caught sight of her stricken face in the mirror. Was she mad? But again the vision of Bryce and Naomi in each other's arms filled her mind, even though she closed her eyes and shook her head violently to make it go away.

There was silence from outside. He did not try the door, which she had not locked anyway. She assumed he had gone away. For several minutes she stood staring at her reflection as though at a stranger. Then she sat down on the bathroom stool, her head in her hands, but she could not weep.

It must have been an hour later that she crept back into the bedroom. The lamp on her side of the bed was on, but Bryce was not in the bed. He had gone. Where? Downstairs to the sofa? No, Betsy might notice him there. He must have gone to another bedroom. She half made up her mind to go and find him, but knew she was still too upset, and he was probably too angry now anyway. It might only make matters worse.

She stood staring at the large double bed with its tumbled bedclothes for a moment or two, and then, almost with a sense of relief she slipped back between the sheets and buried her head in the pillow.

'What am I going to do?' she asked herself with a hopelessness bordering on despair.

CHAPTER SIX

SHARON woke late. Even so she lay for a few minutes in the big empty bed letting the fiasco of the night before wash over her. She went hot and cold as she remembered her flight from Bryce and the sudden wave of revulsion that had engulfed her. But how could she have loved him while believing that he was almost certainly fantasising another woman in his arms?

'Am I mad?' she asked herself, as the minutes ticked inexorably away on the bedside clock. She didn't *know* that he still loved Naomi. Maybe she had made a fuss about nothing.

She would apologise, confess her silly fears, and they would make up and start again. Resolutely, she got up and showered, half expecting Bryce to come hammering on the bathroom door, but he did not appear. The shower had been dry when she entered it, so she supposed he had either used the second bathroom, or was not yet up. When she checked, he was not in any of the other bedrooms.

She quickly dressed and went downstairs where she found, as she expected, Betsy pottering in the kitchen. Sharon wondered if the housekeeper had any suspicion of what had happened last night. Bryce had left no sign of occupancy in any of the bedrooms so Sharon concluded at last that he had probably slept in his study where there was a leather couch. She wondered if he was still there.

Betsy beamed at her cheerfully. 'Good morning, Sharon, my dear! I was just going to come up and give you a call when I heard the shower. Overslept a bit, did you?'

'I'm afraid so.' Sharon took a slice of bread and slid it into the toaster.

'I hope I didn't disturb you when I came back last night,' said Betsy. 'It was quite late when my nephew drove me home, but I came in as quietly as I could.'

'I didn't hear a sound,' said Sharon, which was true.

Betsy poured her a cup of coffee. 'Bryce went off very early. He said he has a hectic programme today.' She sighed. 'He's so dedicated.'

Sharon heaved a silent sigh. So Bryce had left already. He must still be very angry with her not to have wakened her before he left. Or had he realised why she had fled from him last night, and felt guilty about it?

There was a dull ache around her heart as she rushed her meagre breakfast and tried to chat trivialities with Betsy. Fortunately she did not have to contribute much to the conversation. Betsy was happy to talk about her visit to her sister's, exclaim again on how lovely the wedding had been, and even relate an anecdote or two from her own nursing days.

Once she directed a rather steady look at Sharon. 'Now don't you overdo it, my girl. Remember you're a wife first. I hope you're going to think about giving up nursing soon.'

To avoid any argument, Sharon said, 'Yes, Betsy, I expect I will.'

Betsy approved with an eager smile. 'Now that's sensible talk. I knew you'd be the kind to want to settle down and have a family. Can't be too soon for Bryce. That's what he needs, a family of his own.' Her eyes glowed with enthusiasm. 'And I must say I look forward to a bit of baby-sitting in my old age!'

Sharon was glad that she was able to excuse herself before the conversation became too involved, or she gave herself away.

The morning was hectic, with doctors doing their rounds, today with students in tow, consultants popping in, two patients going home, another requiring a brain-scan, and the usual crop of demands from the rest. There was a minor panic when one presumably bored child was not discovered doing it until she had consumed most of the flowers in the vase on her bedside table.

'Melanie just loves flowers,' her mother had said yesterday, arranging the mixed bunch in a squat bowl that she assured Sharon would be difficult to knock over. She had not apparently realised just how much her daughter did relish flowers.

When Sharon discovered her, Melanie was dribbling petals all over her nightdress. She offered one to Sharon, smiling broadly. Eating flowers was not something Sharon would have expected a seven year old to do, but life was full of surprises, she thought ruefully as she insisted on Melanie spitting out the remains of the bloom she was consuming.

A quick check with the Poisons Information Bureau which the hospital ran for the public revealed that none of the vegetation was poisonous, and Sharon sighed with relief. Sister Garland, however, was critical.

'You should be more watchful, Nurse Townshend,' she admonished, adding pointedly, 'You can't nurse efficiently if your mind is on other things.'

Sharon accepted the rebuke meekly and did not point out that she was not the only nurse on duty in the ward, and that what had happened was totally unforeseen. She had to admit that half her mind was elsewhere that morning, and that this was not good. As time went by she began to feel more and more that she had made a complete fool of herself last night, had perhaps alienated Bryce for no good reason at all, and had in fact behaved in a way that could even send him falling back into Naomi's arms.

The conviction that she must see him and explain grew until she could stand the suspense no longer, and certainly could not wait until the evening. So, on her way back from taking a blood sample to Pathology, she decided to look in on her husband, even though this was going against their own rule that they would not seek each other out during hospital hours except on hospital business.

The Cardiology Unit was on the fifth floor, and Sharon's heart thumped nervously as she walked along the corridor towards Bryce's office. She felt more like a prisoner on her way to execution than a bride of two days going to visit her husband. She knew Bryce had had an operation to perform that morning, but she hoped he would be free by now.

As she pushed open one of the double doors leading to the Cardiology Unit, she stopped suddenly. Two people had passed through just ahead of her. Bryce and Naomi Forrest. Sharon stared at their backs, and a wave of jealousy washed over her. Naomi's ringing tones came clearly to her, echoing along the corridor.

'It really is great to be back, Bryce. I'm going to enjoy working together again so much. It'll be just like old times . . . only better.' She laughed, a low vibrant sound. 'Now, you'll have to treat me like an equal instead of an ignorant little woman!'

'You were never ignorant,' he replied, a bit gruffly. 'And I don't believe I ever treated you as though you were.'

She slid her arm through his. 'Only joking . . .' She looked up at his face. 'I'm really impressed by what you're doing here, Bryce, and I'm terribly thrilled to be joining your team. I feel sure we're going to achieve that breakthrough. But you must bring me right up to date with your research. We ought to have a real heart-to-heart . . .' Again her laugh echoed warmly along the corridor '. . . if you'll pardon the terrible pun . . . so that you can put me in the picture. Do you think your charming little wife could spare you for one evening? We could talk without constant interruption then, and make much more progress.'

Progress in what? Sharon thought jealously, as they paused outside a door near Bryce's office. Naomi opened it. Obviously it was a room allocated to her. Neither had noticed Sharon, still poised half way through the swing doors. She remained transfixed and indecisive, not sure whether she had the courage now to speak to Bryce. She did not hear his reply to Naomi's suggestion because at that moment an orderly wheeling a massive linen trolley approached from behind and she was obliged to step aside to let him push through.

'Thanks, love,' he said with a grin.

Sharon retreated, but unfortunately Bryce had seen her, and he called out, 'Sharon . . .'

She was forced to confront him after all. His face was grim as he strode down the corridor towards her. Looking at him she still found it hard to believe she was actually his wife. She twisted the ring on her finger apprehensively.

'Did you want to see me?' he asked, his gaze dark and forbidding as he scrutinised her face. She could not tell whether he was angry with her, or just exasperated.

Panic made her blurt out, 'No . . . no, I didn't come to see you. I was . . . er . . . looking for someone . . . er . . . Dr Fitzgerald.'

Norton's name was the first that came into her mind. It was hardly surprising that Bryce's eyebrows rose a fraction as he queried, 'Up here?'

Sharon felt the colour rushing into her cheeks. She had blundered, but the lie was told and she had to go along with it now. 'Yes,' she said, not quite meeting his eyes. 'Someone . . . said he'd come up here . . . they must have been mistaken.' She managed a carefree smile. 'You haven't seen him then?'

'No.' He folded his arms and regarded her speculatively. 'Perhaps you should try paging him. It might save wasting time looking all over the hospital for him, unless of course you don't want the whole hospital to know you want him.'

His tone was scathing. He knew she was lying, and he probably knew the real reason she was there, but he was refusing to help her. And without some encouragement from him Sharon knew she would make a complete hash of what she wanted to say if she tried now.

'I'd better be getting back,' she said lamely. She added as offhandedly as she could, 'You'll be home for dinner tonight?'

'I expect so,' he answered, rather coolly.

'That's good,' Sharon said. 'See you then.' She turned and left him, certain that he remained staring after her through the swinging glass doors, thinking . . . what?

She realised when she reached for the lift call button that her hands were trembling. It was crazy to have let seeing Bryce and Naomi together unnerve her so that she had gone all to pieces and had been unable to talk to him. He was her husband after all. Just because he and Naomi were going to be working together didn't mean they would resume their old intimacy. She must stop being jealous.

Sharon felt thoroughly exhausted when she reached home in late afternoon. She prowled restlessly about the house, avoiding Betsy who was busy in the kitchen. When Bryce came home, Sharon jumped at the sound of his key in the door and her heart leapt involuntarily. She had been half expecting, she realised, that he would phone and say he would not be home for dinner. Relief surged through her, but she greeted him in as normal a tone as she was able.

'Shall I get you a drink?' she asked, as he slumped into a chair in the drawing room.

'Thanks . . .' He had dropped a casual kiss on her forehead, and now his eyes roved over her in that rather disconcertingly speculative way they had earlier in the day. Again she wished she knew what he was thinking. She went to the cocktail cabinet and opened it.

'Whisky or brandy?' she knew he liked either.

'Brandy, thanks.'

Sharon poured a measure, and a sherry for herself. He sat in an armchair, she sat at one end of a sofa, half hoping he might join her there, that with just a touch, a word, all would be well again and the right atmosphere created for confessions later. But just believing in miracles did not make them happen. There was still considerable constraint between them.

'I must say Betsy makes me feel very lazy.' Sharon was aware as she made the remark, that she had made it before, but she could think of nothing scintillating to say.

'Betsy knows that nurses are very hard-working,' Bryce offered, swirling his brandy reflectively.

'She was telling me this morning a bit about when she was a nursing sister,' said Sharon, glad to talk about Betsy. 'They were a lot less democratic in hospitals in those days.' She added, when he did not comment, 'She was very fond of your parents . . . obviously is of you too. I don't think I shall ever measure up to the standard Betsy considers adequate for your wife.'

'There's no need for self-denigration,' Bryce said shortly, with more impatience than reassurance.

Another silence ensued. Sharon felt she was a total failure as a conversationalist, but the silence was unbearable. As her tension mounted she made a few more trivial remarks, to which he responded politely, but with an air of preoccupation. At last she said, 'I think I'll go and see if Betsy needs a hand.' She glanced at his empty glass. 'Another drink?'

His eyes met hers impassively. 'Don't worry, I'll get it.'

Rebuffed, Sharon hurried out to the kitchen where Betsy was about to dish up the meal.

'And how's that man of yours, Sharon, dear?' the housekeeper inquired, taking the plates out of the warmer.

'A bit tired, I think,' Sharon answered.

Betsy glanced at her with a twinkle. 'Early to bed, eh?'

Sharon flushed faintly, and wished she had not invited the teasing remark. She was sure now that Betsy had no idea that Bryce had not slept in the big bedroom last night.

'You can take it in, dear,' said Betsy, as she put the gravy boat on its saucer. 'The apricot tart's warming in the oven, and I've whipped the cream.'

Sharon hesitated. 'Betsy . . . why won't you eat with us? I know you used to eat with Bryce.'

Betsy fluttered her gnarled hands in dismissal of the idea. 'What do you think I am? I'm not playing gooseberry to you two love-birds. And you've no need to worry about me. I like to be lazy and watch TV with a tray on my knees. Now run along before it gets cold.' She wagged an admonitory finger at Sharon. 'And don't you touch the dishes. Promise?'

Sharon knew it was useless to argue. She would only offend the housekeeper. 'You're very good to us,' she said sincerely. 'But I'm sure Bryce would like you to have some meals with us, and I would too. What about Sunday lunch?'

Betsy looked pleased despite her protests. 'All right,' she conceded. 'But I'm not one to interfere in people's lives. You young people want to be alone. Marriage isn't all a bed of roses. You need time to get to know each other by yourselves. People in your profession never see enough of each other, that's the trouble.'

Sharon gave her a swift, anxious glance. Did she suspect that all was not well after all, and was saying so in a round-about way? There was no time to speculate because Betsy was shooing her out of the kitchen. Before she went off to her flat with her own meal on a tray she poked her head around the dining-room door and said hello to Bryce, who also pressed her to join them (he doesn't want to be alone with me, Sharon thought) but Betsy firmly resisted.

As she went, he chuckled, surprising Sharon because he had been so gloomy since he had come home. 'She's like a clucky hen with a couple of chicks,' he said. 'We mustn't spoil her fun.' His eyes met Sharon's and his expression made her wince. What was it she could see deep in those grey depths . . . pain? . . . regret?

They ate in moody silence. Every time Sharon opened her mouth she could not avoid comparing herself with Naomi. If Naomi were here now, she would be talking with assurance, intelligence and vivacity, and he would be responding. He had said he didn't want to talk shop with her but she suspected he would be only too willing to discuss his ideas with Naomi.

'There's a good programme on TV tonight,' Sharon remarked, as she served the dessert. 'That documentary on China. I missed it the first time it was screened. Do you want to watch it?'

Bryce glanced up. 'No, I don't think I will. I've got some work I want to do, some notes to write up.' His eyes were perfectly steady. 'You watch it, though.'

So Sharon watched television alone while Bryce retired to his study and closed the door, taking his coffee with him. Although she tried to concentrate on the documentary, Sharon's attention persistently wandered and she lost the thread of it all half way through. She must have dropped off finally because when she woke with a start, the programme had changed. She rose and switched off the set. It was eleven o'clock.

Sharon yawned. She felt very weary. It was a tiredness born of emotional upheaval, aggravated by a hectic day at the hospital. For a moment she stood staring at the dead television screen, wondering if Bryce was still working and if she dared disturb him to ask if he would like a cup of coffee. She felt nervous of interrupting him but nevertheless did so, tapping lightly on the study door before tentatively pushing it open.

Bryce glanced up, slightly surprised as she half entered the room. He was sitting on the other side of his big mahogany desk, the one he had told her had belonged to his mother. The angled desk light accentuated the strong uncompromising lines of his jaw and cheekbones, the small lines about his eyes and mouth, and cast his eyes in deep shadow. He looked a little gaunt in the unflattering light, and to Sharon, quite formidable.

'I thought you'd have gone to bed,' he remarked in a flat voice.

'I fell asleep in front of the television,' she answered. 'I wondered if you'd like some coffee.'

'I wouldn't mind, thanks.'

It gave her pleasure to provide this small service for him, and when she carried the tray in, although she had not brought a cup for herself, she hoped he would invite her to join him.

He did not. He merely glanced up briefly and was even more abrupt, if anything, than before. 'Thanks . . .' He glanced at her as dismissively as if she were an orderly bothering him. 'I shall be a while yet. Don't wait up for me.'

Sharon replied sharply, 'I wasn't going to. I'm rather tired. I'm going to bed now.'

'Goodnight,' he said.

Sharon wanted to rush to the other side of the desk and throw her arms around him and kiss him, but his coldness kept her at a distance. She merely said, 'Goodnight, Bryce.'

Sharon drank a cup of coffee alone in the kitchen, staring into space and beating her mind against the wall of frustration she felt. Then she sighed deeply, rinsed her cup and saucer and upturned them on the drainer. What was the use? She might as well let things take their course, which was what they would do, in spite of her.

And with this sense of fatalism sitting heavily on her heart, she went up to bed. She slept almost at once, and deeply. She woke once and realised that she was no longer alone in the wide bed. Bryce must have come to bed some time ago without disturbing her. Momentarily she felt a wild impulse to fling herself across the bed towards him, but she could not bring herself to do it. His manner that evening had been all rejection. She knew she would not be able to bear it if he rejected her now too.

When she woke in the morning, Bryce's broad back still hunched the bedclothes and he was turned away from her, breathing sonorously in deep sleep. Sharon slipped out of bed and went to the bathroom. When she returned to the bedroom a few minutes later, Bryce was awake, lying on his back with his hands behind his head.

'I didn't hear the alarm,' he said.

'You must have been very late last night,' Sharon murmured, drawing on her panty-hose, aware that he was watching every movement as she dressed.

He yawned. 'I was a bit. You were dead to the world. I finished what I wanted to do, to bring Naomi up to date with what I've been working on in the transplant area.' He added as an afterthought. 'Dr Hargreaves, too, when he gets here.'

Sharon swallowed hard. So it had been for Dr Forrest that he had stayed up late last night. She never knew quite why she blurted it out but suddenly she heard herself saying, 'She's beautiful.'

Bryce sprawled his large frame over onto her side of the bed and lay on his side, his head propped on one hand, leaning on his elbow. 'Jealous?' he teased but there was an enigmatic shadow in his eyes.

Sharon caught her breath. 'Have I any reason to be?' She walked quickly to the dressing table and began to brush her hair.

Bryce yawned audibly. 'I suppose I'd better show a leg myself.' The question she had asked hung in the air unanswered.

Sharon watched his reflection in the mirror as he eased his large pyjama-clad frame off the bed and padded across the carpet to the en-suite bathroom. She almost felt relief when the door closed behind him and she heard the shower start.

Downstairs Betsy was bustling about in her usual way.

Sharon breakfasted and left the house without seeing Bryce again.

At lunch time that day, Sharon was sitting by herself in the canteen when Norton Fitzgerald came across and slid into a chair opposite her.

'And how's the blushing bride?'

'Hello, Norton.' Sharon was in no mood for his banter, but her less than cheery response proved a mistake.

'Aye, aye, you look a bit down in the mouth,' he observed, reaching across and holding three fingers under her chin, tilting her face to give her a closer scrutiny. 'What's up?'

'Nothing . . .' It was becoming her catchword, Sharon thought ruefully.

He smiled. 'Come on, you can tell Uncle Norton. He's a man of the world. Bryce not coming up to scratch, is that it? Had a little tiff, have you?'

'No, of course not!' Her response was a little too vehement.

Norton drew his lips together and clicked his tongue. 'Mmm, that tells me that you definitely have. Give me three guesses, and I guarantee to get it in one . . . Dr Forrest.'

Sharon flinched. Why did he have to say it? She struggled valiantly not to show that his perception had found its mark.

'I really don't know what you mean,' she said, with an attempt at innocence.

Norton leaned across the table and in a confidential tone said, 'Tough luck she decided to come back.'

'The Cardiology Unit is bound to benefit,' said Sharon. 'She has the kind of expertise they need.'

'And Cardiology isn't going to be the only beneficiary, I'll bet,' remarked Norton, meaningfully, 'A little bird told me that Bryce used to be crazy about her.'

'The gossip grapevine is evidently very efficient in this hospital,' Sharon answered, rather acidly, adding emphatically. 'They lived together for two years and she left him and went off with someone else, but I suppose your informant told you that.'

Norton's eyes narrowed. 'I wonder why she's come back . . . the real reason I mean. Perhaps she'd heard he was still single and thought he was pining for her.'

'Norton, I think you're being impertinent,' Sharon said forthrightly.

He smiled pityingly. 'Sharon, I don't want to be a pessimist, but you'll need to keep a firm rein on your husband. I just saw her and . . . wow . . . she packs a pretty sensual punch, and I'd say he's Class A unadulterated vulnerable.'

'Now you're being insulting,' Sharon said, incensed. She got up to go even though she had not quite finished her meal. 'You don't know what you're talking about and I'm not sitting here listening to it.'

Norton grasped her hand and forced her back into her seat. 'Sorry, love, I didn't mean to be brutal, but you might as well face facts. There are those who think he wouldn't have married you if he'd known she was coming back in time.'

'Of course he knew,' she retorted.

Norton said slowly, looking steadily at her. 'Well, maybe he did it to spite her.'

'I think you're despicable!' Sharon exclaimed, but there were painful echoes of the words spoken by that woman at the wedding in Norton's remark. Was it what everyone now believed?

'I don't want to see my pretty little Rose of Sharon hurt more than she needs to be,' Norton said slowly.

'I am not *your* anything!' hissed Sharon, goaded beyond endurance. 'Let go of my hand!'

Norton refused to do so and Sharon, short of making a scene, had no alternative but to remain where she was. He said earnestly, 'Sharon, you're angry because you don't want to face up to the truth. You hate me for daring to say what's in your own mind. Well, I've got broad shoulders.' His voice was soft, as he leaned forward close to her. 'Broad enough for having a good cry on any time you want.'

Sharon felt like crying right then, but not on his shoulder. She gritted her teeth and said in a chilly tone. 'I've got to go.'

His fingers squeezed hers. 'Wait . . . look who's just come in. Over on the other side.'

Despite herself, Sharon turned her head. She saw Bryce and Naomi entering. Bryce's hand was on the woman doctor's elbow, and she was smiling into his face with complete self assurance.

Sharon looked quickly away. She caught Norton's triumphant look and it, more than what she had seen, infuriated her.

'See,' he said softly. 'She's got a head start, Sharon, and she's ruthless, I can tell. If she wants him, she'll get him.' He released her hand. 'Are you sure you're in love with him? Are you sure it wasn't just flattery that made you say yes?'

In any other circumstances Sharon would have slapped his face. Instead, she said, 'How dare you speak to me like this! What do you know about anything?'

'Sharon, darling, it's the chief topic of conversation in this hospital already—how long will the Townshend marriage last? Oh, you and Bryce won't hear the gossip, the subjects of gossip are usually the last to hear, but right from the start people were surprised at the match. You know that. And now . . . well, it does rather look as though Bryce has either made a blunder or is using you. Everyone is agog to see how long it will be before the balloon goes up.'

'I think it's hateful!'

'I know . . . it is, but you're a fool if you go around with blinkers on. I don't want to hurt you, and I don't like you hating me. I'm only thinking of you, Sharon.'

'Very kind of you, I'm sure,' said Sharon sarcastically.

Norton shrugged. 'It's your life . . . But I warn you,

before long he'll start working longer hours, staying out late at night, making excuses . . . and you'll find he's not at the hospital when he said he was going to be, then one day he'll break the sad news that it was all a dreadful mistake.'

Sharon stood up again and this time Norton did not detain her. Tight-lipped, she looked down at him with distaste, flinching at the pity in his eyes. He rose too and with his hand comfortingly around her shoulders accompanied her from the canteen. Sharon vowed she would not look in the direction of Bryce and Naomi, but at the last minute she weakened and stole a glance at their table. The two dark heads were bent close together. Bryce was using his hands expressively to make a point, and Naomi's gaze was fixed attentively on his face. Sharon wondered if her husband had even noticed that his wife was in the canteen.

That afternoon, as her shift was ending, there was a phone call for Sharon. To her surprise it was Bryce.

'Sharon? I thought I might catch you before you left.' There was a slight pause and then he said apologetically, 'I'm afraid I won't be home for dinner tonight.'

'Why not?' Sharon answered, and could almost see Norton grinning triumphantly before her eyes.

She waited for him to offer a manufactured excuse, but he didn't. He said, 'Naomi wants to discuss the notes I compiled, in relation to her work in America. We hope to find a fresh starting point.'

For his work or their relationship? Sharon thought bitterly.

'Shouldn't you be waiting for Dr Hargreaves?' she asked pointedly.

'Well, of course we'll be having a lot of discussions then,' Bryce said easily, 'but Naomi is keen . . .'

'For you to take her out to dinner,' Sharon broke in, trying to disguise the edge to her voice with an overlay of laughter.

'Well, actually she's suggested a meal at her place.'

'Her place?'

'She moved into a flat Sir Leslie organised for her in Toorak, yesterday. I said she was probably in a muddle but she insisted she'd rather talk at home quietly.' He added in a tone that sounded sarcastic, but couldn't have been. 'I didn't think you'd mind.'

'Of course I don't mind,' Sharon replied, the chill around her heart reflected in her voice.

'See you later then,' Bryce said.

Sharon replaced the receiver. The whole hospital, Norton had said, was watching with bated breath to see what would happen, how long the Townshend marriage would last. The senior surgeon and the staff nurse—doomed to failure from the beginning. A mis-match if ever there was one, even if Naomi Forrest hadn't come back. Sharon shuddered convulsively. Already she was an object of pity and she hated it.

Perhaps I ought to walk out right now and leave them to it, she thought as she pedalled home, but she knew she would not do that. Not yet anyway. She would wait until Bryce told her it was over. Over? It hadn't even begun. Wryly she thought of the mockery her marriage was. She'd been a fool to think he had wanted her for herself.

After dinner alone with Betsy, Sharon felt she could not stay in the house all evening wondering when Bryce would come home, imagining him with Naomi, so she rang Janna and asked herself over, taking a cab to the block of flats where she had lived so recently.

Janna was delighted to see her. 'I was dying to tell you the news on the phone,' she said, 'but I thought I'd wait till you got here.'

'What news?' Janna's ebullience acted like a tonic and Sharon's spirits rose a little. 'Tell me!'

'All in good time,' teased Janna. She peered hard at Sharon. 'You're looking peaky.' She giggled. 'I hope you're not . . .' She rolled her eyes in mock dismay.

'If you mean pregnant,' retorted Sharon, 'of course I'm not! I've only been married a few days.'

'Oops, *faux pas*, sorry,' amended Janna with an irrepressibly teasing look, 'But you did get hitched in rather a rush and you know what people are. I bet the Gargoyle for one is watching your waistline like a Victorian grandmother.'

Sharon was shocked. 'Are people really saying that we had to get married?' At least Norton had spared her that embarrassment.

'No . . . well, there's always some snide character who thinks everyone is as careless as they are . . . forget I said it, it wasn't nice . . . and I apologise. Sick joke.' She waltzed towards the kitchen. 'Like a shandy?'

'Thanks.' Sharon looked around at the familiar surroundings and knew a momentary pang of nostalgia. She'd had a lot of fun living here. It was very different from the East Melbourne house. She didn't really feel she belonged there.

Janna came back with the drinks. She seemed to be bubbling over with excitement tonight.

'What are you going to tell me?' Sharon asked, flopping onto the couch. 'I'm dying of curiosity.'

Janna laughed, waving her left hand about. 'You haven't noticed! Sharon, where are your wits?'

Sharon suddenly became aware of the diamond ring glittering on her friend's finger. Janna had always worn a lot of rings and she simply hadn't noticed that this one was on the third finger.

'Janna!' She almost spilt her shandy.

Janna sat beside her and held out the ring for inspection. 'Not bad, is it? We went shopping at lunchtime today. I think it was your wedding that finally tipped the scales.'

'I'm so glad,' Sharon said, happy for Janna, but with a strange empty feeling inside her. Janna would be happy with Peter. The certain knowledge seemed to make the abysmal failure of her marriage to Bryce worse than ever. Janna and Peter had been going together for a couple of years. They knew each other inside out. They were in love. If only, as Norton had suggested, she wasn't really in love with Bryce . . . But she was.

She raised her glass. 'This ought to be champagne, but good luck anyway. I know you'll be very happy, Janna.'

'Are you?' Janna asked, with a penetrating look.

'Yes, of course!'

Janna sipped her drink and put it down. 'Don't let what busybodies are saying come between you,' she advised. 'Naomi Forrest doesn't stand a germ's chance in a steriliser with Bryce now. That fire is well and truly extinguished, I feel sure.'

Sharon smiled gratefully. Janna was doing her best to be reassuring, and she wished she could believe her. But Janna didn't really know anything about it.

'Why isn't Peter here tonight,' she asked, 'seeing you got engaged today?'

Janna heaved a resigned sigh. 'Night school! I wouldn't let him miss it, not even for me.' She smirked. 'When he's got his business management diploma I'm hoping he'll be able to keep me in the manner to which I shall rapidly become accustomed!'

Sharon laughed. Janna was incorrigible.

'And now,' Janna said, 'before I forget, about this fund-raising . . .'

Sharon decided she might as well throw herself wholeheartedly into the fund-raising activities for the hospital. It might help to take her mind off her problems. When you feel low, her mother had often said, do something for someone else, and you'll feel better straight away.

Janna, whose livewire personality ensured that she was a frontline operator in any activity was delighted at Sharon's willingness to lend a hand at more than merely pushing a hospital bed to the City Square and collecting donations en route.

It was after midnight when Sharon phoned for a cab. 'I'll never get up in the morning,' she wailed when she saw the time.

To her surprise, Bryce was already home and waiting up for her. He looked, she thought, a bit distraught, as though something had happened to disturb his composure. She knew it could only be Naomi.

'Where have you been?' His voice was sharply interrogatory.

'I went to see Janna,' she answered.

'That was a sudden decision, wasn't it?' he said suspiciously.

'Well, as you were going to be out, I thought it was a good opportunity.'

He was searching her face as though he didn't believe her. She rushed on, 'Janna and Peter got engaged today.' She yawned. 'I stayed longer than I meant to, you know what Janna is. I feel whacked.' She looked at him levelly. His manner puzzled her, but perhaps it was because he was tense. 'Was your evening a success?'

'Success . . . yes, I suppose so. We talked around a few ideas.' He laughed suddenly, a harsh kind of laugh. 'Naomi hasn't changed much. She's still ambitious, and I doubt if she'll ever let anything stand in her way.'

Sharon averted her face so that he wouldn't read her expression. 'I'm going to bed,' she said.

When she came out of the bathroom, Bryce was sitting on the edge of the bed. He faced her with an anxious expression. 'We can't go on like this, Sharon,' he said at last. The words seemed to be dragged out of him.

Sharon felt the bands tightening around her heart. No, not now, don't tell me now, she screamed inside. She said, quite calmly, 'I suppose not.'

'I think we'd better have a serious talk,' he said. 'Sharon . . .'

She couldn't bear it. 'Not now, Bryce, please . . .' she said hastily. 'I'm terribly tired and it's very late.' It was cowardly, she knew, but she felt so vulnerable at that moment. Her feelings were too close to the surface and she didn't want him to know how deeply he was hurting her.

He sighed. 'Very well . . .' He moved off her side of the bed. 'I'd sleep in the spare room but Betsy might wonder . . .'

She did not answer. She crept into bed and turned her head into the pillow. Presently she felt him crawl into the other side of the big bed. It seemed like a mile between them, but the emotional gulf was wider than their physical separation. She longed for him to take her in his arms, but knew that he never would now.

CHAPTER SEVEN

SHARON was glad when she was rostered for night shifts for a fortnight. It meant she saw less of Bryce. After his attempt to talk to her on the night she had visited Janna and he had spent the evening with Naomi, he did not mention the subject again. This surprised Sharon, especially as he had been so anxious to talk to her then.

Since she could never bring herself to initiate the discussion it remained a barrier between them, while to all intents and purposes life went on normally. They lived together in the same house, and slept in the same bed—although not together temporarily because of Sharon's night shifts. Bryce even kept up a pretence of affection by occasionally kissing her—but never again with passion, and usually only in front of Betsy. He was clearly anxious that Betsy should believe that all was well, at least for the time being. Sometimes Sharon almost believed it herself, at others she would become tense and wonder how long she would be able to tolerate the situation. Why do I tolerate it at all? she asked herself, and the answer was always the same—deep down she nurtured, in spite of everything, a faint hope that Bryce would get over his infatuation for Naomi, or she would reject him again. There was another reason. She loved him, and it seemed that not even his infidelity could change that.

Fortunately a lot of Sharon's spare time was taken up with preparations for the hospital fund-raising week which was fast approaching, and this helped to prevent her from brooding overmuch. Bryce was always gone when she arrived home from the hospital, and often he had not come home before she left again in the evenings. Because he had insisted, she had agreed to travel to and from the hospital by taxi, except when she was on an early shift and could cycle both ways in daylight. She had protested strongly when he had first suggested the taxi, but he had been adamant about her taking one at night.

'I am not having my wife gadding about at night on a bicycle,' he had stated firmly. 'It's not safe. You can take a taxi until you get yourself a car.'

Sharon had made some remark about the cost of taxis and he had retorted instantly: 'For heaven's sake, Sharon, I can afford it!'

Not wanting to turn the disagreement into a major row, she had agreed to take taxis while she was on night shift, but had put off the decision about buying a car. She felt too uneasy about everything to do anything so positive, and she was a little surprised that Bryce, in the circumstances, had suggested it.

The explanation suggested itself out of the blue one day when, despite her resolve not too, she was brooding over her marriage, and wondering why Bryce had never again tried to talk to her about it. All at once she stumbled on a possible answer. Naomi had not wanted to get married the first time round. There was no reason why she should have changed. Perhaps Bryce, realising this, had decided that it would suit him better to maintain the facade of marriage, while having Naomi too.

That thought made Sharon so angry she was on the point of accusing him of it on one of her days off when they were both at home for dinner, but just as she was about to launch forth, Naomi telephoned, and by the time Bryce had finished speaking to her, Sharon had lost her courage.

Once or twice she ventured to ask him how his research was progressing, but he was never very forthcoming, answering her with a brisk, 'We're making progress,' or a shrug and, 'These things take time.'

Occasionally they went out to dinner, or entertained

at home. For Sharon these occasions were always a strain, firstly because she felt out of her depth and then because Naomi was usually there. Having Naomi to the house was especially aggravating. Noami would look around her with a distinctly proprietorial air. On her first visit she said to Bryce, in Sharon's hearing, 'I see nothing has changed much.' She shot Sharon a look of smug satisfaction.

Fortunately Bryce was not keen on going out too often. When he was not absorbed in his work, he would take time off to play golf, but Sharon did not join him in this, although before they were married he had suggested she learn to play. He had not mentioned it since. Their limited social life did not bother Sharon. It saved having to pretend to other people that all was well. Bryce obviously thought so too.

Although Sharon did not altogether welcome his attentions, Norton Fitzgerald hovered around and sought her out on every possible excuse, it seemed. Since the occasion in the canteen when she had become very angry with him for being personal, he had avoided the subject of Bryce and in fact never mentioned either him or Naomi, or offered any hospital gossip. Despite herself, Sharon found some solace in talking to him, and so long as he did not overstep the line of friendship she did not rebuff him.

Sometimes he drove her home at the end of her shift, and often he buttonholed her in the canteen. They always found plenty to talk about because Norton was involved in the fund-raising almost as much as Sharon. But when he casually suggested taking her to the races on her day off, Sharon, although tempted because such a diversion would take her out of herself, always refused. She had no wish to become involved with Norton.

Janna's preoccupation with the fund-raising did not prevent her from noticing that Sharon was often in Norton's company and one day, rather to Sharon's astonishment, she said disapprovingly:

'Whenever I see you nowadays, you've got Dr Fitz-gerald in tow.'

Sharon stared at her. 'I don't like the way you put that, Janna. We're both involved in the fund-raising . . .'

Janna's eyes narrowed a fraction. 'I hope that's all you're involved in.'

Sharon went pink. 'I don't know what you mean.'

'Hospitals are hot-beds of gossip,' remarked Janna darkly.

Sharon pursed her lips. As though she didn't know that! But this was something new. 'Who's been saying things about me?' she demanded.

'Nobody,' Janna hastened to reassure her. 'I expect I'm the only one that's noticed, but . . . well, you do seem to be seeing quite a lot of Norton, and . . .' She shrugged. 'Bryce might not like it.'

Sharon smiled wryly. 'There's nothing between Nor-ton and me, Janna, if that's what you're hinting at.'

'I wasn't,' said Janna, giving her a straight look. 'But there's something odd about you lately. 'You're . . . preoccupied . . .'

'Maybe I am,' retorted Sharon, feeling edgy, 'but there's no need to jump to conclusions. I didn't think you'd do that, Janna.'

'Sorry,' said Janna at once. 'Opened my big mouth too wide as usual. Don't let's quarrel about it, Sharon.' She eyed her friend speculatively for a moment, then added anxiously, 'Are you sure everything's all right.'

Sharon summoned a bright laugh. 'Of course it is!' She had no intention of admitting to anyone, not even Janna, that her marriage was a failure. But even as she spoke she had the feeling that Janna was not convinced.

However, her former flatmate reined in her natural tendency to forthrightness and did not pursue the sub-ject. Sharon felt sure she was dying to mention Naomi to see what reaction that would draw from her friend, but was not prepared to go that far and perhaps anger Sharon. Sharon wondered what Janna had heard about

Naomi and Bryce. She was sure there was gossip circulating in the hospital but no-one was tactless enough to repeat it to her. Not even Janna.

The day of the hospital-bed marathon was a day off for both Sharon and Janna, as they were actively participating, along with a number of other nurses. Rosters had been stretched and squeezed to allow as many nursing staff as possible to participate without upsetting hospital routines, and many had given up their days off to aid the cause.

At first Sharon almost wished she hadn't volunteered. She felt rather foolish pushing a bed along, but everyone else seemed a bit sheepish at the start too. However, they soon warmed to the task, and eventually it turned into an occasion for a great deal of hilarity.

The traffic had been diverted and the route was posted with smiling policemen to make sure all went smoothly. There was plenty of good-natured banter from passers-by, plenty of teasing, wolf-whistles and laughter, but most gratifying was that people gave generously and by the time the procession reached the City Square, breathless with laughter, and turning it into a race at the finish, the bedpans and other more conventional collecting boxes were jingling with coins in a very satisfying way.

In the crowded City Square during the lunch hour and most of the afternoon, the nurses in their crisp white uniforms mingled with the shoppers and office workers and rattled their collection boxes. Donations flowed in, and it was an exuberant Janna who, back at the hospital later, exclaimed:

'What a day! I reckon we doubled the target.'

She and several of the volunteers were hastily counting the money they had collected so that the total could be announced at the ball that night, the finale to the week of fund-raising for the hospital.

'Have you got a new dress for the ball?' Janna asked Sharon, as they were preparing to go home to get ready for the evening.

Sharon nodded. 'Yes. Have you?'

Janna made a face. 'Nope. Can't afford it. Peter says we can't get married until he's qualified and we've saved the deposit for a house, so no new dresses at the moment.' She grinned. 'I'm not crying. I've got stacks of clothes. I was always extravagant.' She looked suddenly dreamy. 'Funny how you can change.'

Sharon laughed. Janna certainly had changed. She felt almost guilty not having to worry about spending money on a new dress. She hadn't had to save up for the deposit on a house. She had walked straight into Bryce's beautiful house. But Janna would still have more than she had, she reflected sadly, as she waited for Norton who had promised to give her a lift home.

Bryce was already at home when she arrived. He looked a trifle distracted.

'How was the day?' he asked, a bit abruptly.

'Great,' said Sharon. 'Janna says we've more than doubled the target, but she'll have to re-check. I'm a bit late because we were getting a figure to be announced at the ball tonight.'

'Who brought you home?' Bryce inquired.

'Norton.'

He said no more about the day's fund-raising and presently Sharon went upstairs to change. Bryce said he would follow in a few minutes. Sharon's new dress was hanging on the wardrobe and it had, she knew, been lovingly pressed by Betsy. Sharon surveyed it gloomily, and half wished they weren't going to the ball. It would be an ordeal, she knew. That was partly why she had splashed out on this rather expensive new dress. She had hoped it might lift her flagging morale. It was also in defiance of Naomi, even though she knew perfectly well that Dr Forrest was bound to win hands down in the glamour stakes.

Sharon knew a moment of gratification when Bryce saw her dressed. He came out of the bathroom after his shower, a towel around his waist, his hair glistening wet, and Sharon, catching a glimpse of him in the mirror as she applied mascara, felt a swift catch at her heart. Then she saw the sudden flash of spontaneous admiration in his eyes, but it vanished as quickly as it had come, and there remained only a rather strained set to his mouth.

When he said, 'Very seductive . . .' there was faint sarcasm in his voice.

He stood behind her for a moment and placed his hands on her shoulders, bare but for the narrow straps of the deep red satin gown that revealed a tantalising amount of bosom and clung sensuously to the rest of her slender figure. For a second his fingers stiffened in a brief grip, and she thought he was steeling himself to say something right away. Instantly she panicked and shrugged him away.

'Don't jog me . . . I'll smudge mascara all over my face.'

He moved abruptly away and began to dress. He looked exceedingly handsome, she thought, in the maroon velvet jacket that was almost the same shade as her dress, and black trousers, and it made her heart constrict just to look at him.

'Can you tie these?' he asked, after a long tussle with a new maroon bow tie. 'There's something peculiar about this one.'

Sharon tied it for him, steeling herself not to fling her arms around his neck and cling to him as she did so.

'Why don't you buy the sort that are already tied?' she asked, manipulating the ends deftly.

'I don't like cheating,' he said.

Sharon flinched. Didn't he? Wasn't he cheating her now? She pulled the bow taut and arranged the folds and ends neatly. 'I think that'll do. I hope it won't come undone!'

By the time they arrived at the reception centre where the ball was being held, the car park was almost full, but Bryce managed to spot a parking place. It was a balmy night, and the setting, on the river bank, was picturesque and quite romantic, Sharon thought, a shade wistfully.

In the ballroom, there was already quite a crowd and couples were dancing to the music of a five-piece orchestra at one end. At the other was a rock band which was to alternate with it. Sharon suddenly felt nervous. Tonight she would be mingling with a different set of people, not the nurses she worked with and their boyfriends, but surgeons, specialists and consultants and their wives. There would also be a sprinkling of VIPs from both the medical and non-medical worlds. She felt as she always had at the few dinner parties they had been to, out of her depth.

Bryce had arranged to join a party of his colleagues, and soon after their arrival Sharon found herself absorbed into a small group of mainly middle-aged men and women, some of whom she knew slightly. The women were all beautifully gowned and obviously fresh from the hairdresser's. Sharon was glad she had given way to extravagance for once when buying her own dress. The worst moment was when Naomi appeared. She was accompanied by a tall, distinguished man with almost white hair and piercing blue eyes.

'Sir Leslie Ponting,' Bryce said in a low voice to Sharon.

Naomi and her escort joined the party. Introductions were made and Sharon, slightly amused, caught a bold glance from Sir Leslie as he looked her over approvingly.

'Delightful, Townshend, delightful,' he boomed. 'Wise man, marrying a young wife. Keeps you on your mettle. Does you the world of good to have a bit of glamour about you.'

'Really, Uncle Les,' interposed Naomi, laughing throatily, 'Bryce isn't all that old!' She fluttered her lashes at Bryce and winked at him.

As Sharon had expected, Naomi was exquisitely gowned. Her dress was of gold and white satin with filmy draperies from the shoulders caught at the waist with a gold sash. She would have looked, Sharon thought, like a Greek goddess if her hair had not been so short. Gold earrings and a gold bracelet added a touch of opulence to the ensemble.

She said loudly, 'I'm surprised at you, Bryce, allowing your wife to make a spectacle of herself today. I mean, riding a bicycle to work is bad enough, but is it really "done" for a senior surgeon's wife to trundle a hospital bed down the high road, and flourish a bedpan in the City Square!' Her tone was light and teasing, but Sharon sensed a barb behind the words.

She felt the colour rising into her cheeks and suddenly wished she had not participated today. Bryce had not objected and it had never occurred to her that anyone would think it undignified. But would Naomi have done it? Obviously not. As Bryce's wife she would have regarded herself as above such carrying-on. Sharon glanced at him. Did he think she had let him down?

He said mildly, 'Why should I mind? Sharon can do whatever she likes.'

Sir Leslie said quite sharply, 'The trouble with you, Naomi, is that you're a frightful snob.' He smiled at her to soften the rebuke.

'I think it's very sporting of those young women to support the hospital so wholeheartedly,' put in one of the other men. 'I hope you collected a lot of money.'

'Yes, we did,' said Sharon. 'It was a record, I believe.'

The rather plump middle-aged wife of the doctor who had spoken said with a laugh, 'And it's all good fun. I only wish I still had the figure and energy to participate.' Her remark was laughingly supported by the other wives.

Sharon relaxed. Naomi, however, was not a bit put out by being very firmly squashed. She turned to Bryce and said:

'What are we sitting around here for? Bryce, aren't you going to dance with me? I know Uncle Les is dying to chat up your wife.'

My name is Sharon, Sharon thought in a burst of annoyance. Does she have to refer to me as though I'm just one of his possessions. She half hoped Bryce would insist on dancing first with her, but Naomi's charm was powerful. The next moment they were on the floor, and she was being led after them by a determined Sir Leslie Ponting.

'I'm old fashioned, I'm afraid,' he apologised, as he gallantly piloted Sharon onto the dance floor. 'I don't think my old bones could stand up to the shaking up of some of these new-fangled dances.'

He clasped Sharon tightly in a regulation dancing-class hold, and manoeuvred her expertly through a gap in the dancers on the edge of the floor towards the emptier centre of the ballroom.

Sharon was surprised at his agility and the superb sense of rhythm he demonstrated.

'You dance beautifully, Sir Leslie,' she said, as he whirled her around expertly.

He smiled, his pale blue eyes flattering her, as he executed a few more intricate steps, then whirled her round again. Then he said abruptly, 'What do you think of Dr Forrest, eh?'

Taken aback, Sharon answered falteringly, 'I . . . I don't know her very well.' She endeavoured to be non-committal. 'She's a brilliant surgeon, so I hear.'

'Too brilliant for her own good,' stated the elderly scientist. 'My god-daughter, you know?'

Sharon nodded. 'Yes. You must be very proud of her.'

'Hmmph,' he replied, 'I sometimes wonder if I did the right thing putting her through medical school. Her parents died, you know, when she was a teenager. She lived with Doris—my late wife—and me for a few years. We spoilt her I'm afraid.' There was a slight pause and then he added candidly, 'I never thought it would last, her and Bryce. She's too ambitious, too independent. Still is.' He peered shrewdly at Sharon. 'Are you ambitious?'

Sharon shrugged. 'Not really. I'm happy doing what I am doing.'

'Which is?'

'I'm on Children's Surgical.'

The incisive eyes burned into hers. 'Ah, yes. You like kids, do you?'

'Yes, I always wanted to work with children,' Sharon admitted. 'I was going to be a kindergarten teacher at first, but somehow I fell into nursing instead. My father's a doctor so I suppose that had something to do with it.'

It was easy to talk to Sir Leslie. Despite the brusqueness of his manner, there was an underlying kindness that encouraged confidences. Sharon understood why Bryce regarded him so highly, not just as a professional, but as a person.

After a few minutes Sir Leslie admitted to breathlessness and they returned to the table where, for a short while, they were alone.

'Not as young as I used to be,' Sir Leslie remarked. 'Used to dance all night once.' He flashed her a youthful smile, then returned to their former conversation. 'Your father's a doctor, you said. Where? In Melbourne?'

Sharon soon found herself telling him about her family and he listened with apparent interest, nodding every now and then to encourage her. At last she said apologetically, 'I'm sorry . . . I must be boring you.'

'Of course you're not boring me,' he boomed, and with a twinkle added, 'Your face lights up when you're talking about things that matter to you, and besides a beautiful woman is never boring.' The gimlet eyes searched her face. 'Why did you marry Bryce?'

Sharon drew a sharp breath. He was looking intently at her, waiting for and expecting an answer—a truthful one.

'Because . . . because I fell in love with him,' she said, barely above a whisper.

'Not because you thought it would be fun being a

surgeon's wife? Because you thought Bryce was a good catch?'

Sharon's cheeks flooded with angry colour. 'No, of course not! How dare . . .' She stopped, aware that she ought not to be rude to him even if he was to her.

Sir Leslie slapped his hand on her knee and laughed delightedly. 'I love the way a woman looks when she is indignant . . . especially when it's genuine.' His voice dropped to a confidential whisper. 'I hope Bryce knows how lucky he is marrying a nice girl like you.' He patted her knee again. 'Take my advice and start a family just as soon as you can. Bryce needs a family. He's been a bachelor too long.'

Sharon flinched, not because she felt he was being too personal but because what he had advised would never happen. For one moment she was tempted to confess the truth to him, sure that Sir Leslie Ponting would be a sympathetic listener, but he spoke again before she could begin.

'You're not jealous of Naomi, I hope,' he asked point blank.

'No . . .' It didn't sound convincing, and Sharon feared she had not fooled this astute old man.

'Try not to be,' he advised wisely. 'It's what she wants. There's nothing surer than jealousy to drive two people apart. I'll be frank with you, my dear. Naomi doesn't want Bryce, she only wants to take him away from you. It boosted her ego to think he had not married and she got a nasty shock when she discovered he had. She isn't the marrying kind but she's jealous of people who are and make a success of it. Specially Bryce. She's making a play for him again, silly child, and I've told her she's making a fool of herself but she won't listen. Complex girl . . .' He sighed, 'But she has her good points.' A smile lit his face, 'Even if flattering an old man who knows she's doing it is one of them! But don't you worry, Sharon, Bryce is no fool.'

Sharon did not know what to say. It was kind of the old

man to try to reassure her, but like Janna, wasn't he just deceiving himself as well as her? They had both under-estimated the powerful attraction between Bryce and Naomi.

As Sir Leslie finished speaking, the rest of the party began drifting back, and Sharon saw Bryce and Naomi bringing up the rear, she clinging to his arm, looking at him, seeming to hang on his every word. They looked good together, she admitted reluctantly, and wished she didn't feel so jealous.

Suddenly she felt the need for a brief respite, so she stood up and excused herself. To her annoyance, Naomi instantly said, 'Are you going to the powder room?'

Sharon nodded.

'I'll come too,' Naomi said, placing her hand on Bryce's knee as she got up.

A few moments later, as they stood side by side at the powder room mirrors touching up lipstick and powder, Naomi said, 'That's a divine dress, Sharon.' She blotted her lips on a tissue and turned to look Sharon over minutely. There was no admiration in her eyes, however-er.

'Thank you,' Sharon murmured, surprised at the com-pliment, hollow though it was.

Naomi, inclining her head in a reflective way, added, 'But isn't it just a teeny bit . . . well, provocative for a surgeon's wife?' Her eyes glittered in the artificial light and her smooth skin glowed. She was really very beauti-ful, but so hard.

Sharon was too taken aback to reply immediately.

'Don't get me wrong,' said Naomi, silkily. 'I'm not criticising. It was just that I thought . . . well, you do have a different sort of image to uphold now, and Bryce doesn't like women who flaunt themselves.'

Sharon was stunned. Flaunt herself! The dress was low cut and showed her bare shoulders and back, but it was modest enough, more modest in fact than Naomi's own slinky gown which was slit to the thigh and whose filmy draperies showed quite tantalisingly that she was not wearing a bra.

Sharon said coldly. 'Bryce didn't object.'

Naomi smiled knowingly. 'I don't suppose he would . . . not in so many words. He's not the nagging type. But he broods on things . . . as you'll learn.' She became confidential. 'I could tell you a lot about Bryce, what he likes and doesn't like . . .'

'Thanks,' interrupted Sharon, sharply, 'but I think I'd rather find out for myself.'

Naomi was only momentarily taken aback by Sharon's asperity. Clearly she had expected Bryce's wife to be eager for her advice. She shrugged. 'I was only trying to be helpful. I do after all know Bryce rather better than you do.' The glittering eyes regarded Sharon rather insolently. Naomi did not doubt that she would win, Sharon thought.

Incensed by the woman's attitude, she moved to the door, 'I'm not sure that you do,' she replied. 'You knew him in different circumstances. I'm his wife.' She laid deliberate emphasis on the final phrase.

Naomi allowed a swift flicker of uncertainty to cross her lovely face. Sharon was bolder than she had expected. But as they went out of the powder room she had the last word, as she always would, Sharon thought grimly.

'Who, like Caesar's wife, must be seen to be above reproach,' she murmured, and the look she directed at Sharon was unmistakably malicious.

It was with a sense of relief that Sharon rejoined their party and sat down again between Bryce and Sir Leslie. Naomi immediately engaged Bryce in a conversation that seemed to be a continuation of what they had been discussing on the dance floor earlier, so Sharon was obliged to chat to Sir Leslie. Both were drawn into a conversation amongst the other members of the party and for some minutes there was a lively exchange of views across the table on the ethical problems raised by in vitro fertilisation methods—or test-tube babies as newspaper headlines preferred to call the new development. It was noticeable, that despite the liveliness of the debate, Bryce and Naomi remained absorbed in their own conversation, and seemingly oblivious to the rest. They were speaking in low tones and Sharon could not hear what it was all about.

She was somewhat surprised when Bryce suddenly turned to her and said, 'Come on, our turn now,' and she realised that he meant he wanted to dance with her.

Briefly a warm glow suffused her, and when they were on the dance floor and his arms were around her, she wished they could waltz right out of the ballroom and away from everything and everybody, especially Naomi, to somewhere they could be alone together . . .

'My wife seems to be turning a few heads besides Sir Leslie's,' remarked Bryce after a silence.

She glanced at him. 'People are curious about your wife.'

'More than curious,' said Bryce rather drily. 'Norton Fitzgerald, for instance, is devouring you with lascivious eyes at this very moment.'

'Norton . . .'

'Yes, your friend, Norton,' he said.

Sharon frowned. Perhaps he did disapprove of her dress. Perhaps he did think it was too provocative for a wife. Naomi's was even more so, but maybe that was all right for a . . . Sharon hesitated over thinking the word that had slipped into her mind . . . mistress.

Bryce's voice broke into her thoughts. 'You seem to have made a very good impression on Sir Leslie.'

'I like him very much,' said Sharon, glad to change the subject. 'He's very straightforward, though.'

'He's usually very perceptive. What were you talking about?'

'Oh, this and that . . .' She wondered what Sir Leslie had said to Bryce when she and Naomi were in the powder room. Something perceptive about her? Whatever it might have been Bryce gave the impression that he didn't believe it.

He went on, 'I'm not much of a dancer, I'm afraid. I was never very keen on the sport but one has to make an effort at this sort of do.'

'I'm not all that keen on dancing myself,' admitted Sharon.

'I thought you were. You used to go to discos with Janna,' he reminded her.

'Not all that often. I enjoy dancing . . . but I'm not wild about it,' she said.

He looked unconvinced. 'Nevertheless, I imagine you'd rather be up at the other end with your young friends right now.'

She had not expected a remark like that. 'I don't see why. I'm not all that young, Bryce. I'm twenty-five, remember.'

He half smiled. 'Perhaps you just seem so much younger sometimes . . .'

Sharon bit her lip. Of course she did . . . compared with Naomi. She wasn't sophisticated like Naomi. To him she must seem very ordinary and immature.

They danced rather stiffly, the tension between them almost palpable, and when they returned to their table, Sharon felt the beginnings of a headache. She longed for the evening to end. She was offered some relief however when a few minutes later Norton asked her to dance.

'You can spare Mrs Townshend for one dance I hope,' he said to Bryce. He smiled winningly. 'You won't mind if I steal her back for a short while? All her friends at the other end of the ballroom want to say hello.'

'By all means,' Bryce said generously. It was very obvious that he did not like Norton, and this wasn't the first time Sharon had been made aware of it. She wondered why. Perhaps it was just because Norton was inclined to be flippant and frivolous.

'Pheew . . . bet you're glad of a break from that lot,' said Norton, as he whirled Sharon onto the dance floor, steering her purposefully down towards the other end of the ballroom where most of the people she knew well were gathered at several tables in a large party, and were obviously enjoying themselves.

'What's wrong with them?' Sharon retorted, nettled.

He made a face at her. 'A bit stuffy . . .'

'I don't think so,' Sharon said. 'I had a most interesting conversation with Sir Leslie Ponting.'

Norton raised his eyebrows. 'Oh, pardon me . . . name-dropping now are we?'

Sharon stopped. 'Look, if you're going to keep having a dig at me, why did you bother to ask me to dance? I might as well go straight back.'

At that moment the orchestra ceased playing and couples began to drift off the dance floor.

Norton flung his arms around her. 'Sorry . . . sorry . . . sorry . . .' His eyes met hers and pleaded with her. He smiled coaxingly. 'Just jealous, that's all!'

Sharon wriggled furiously in his grasp, conscious that several people were looking at them. Fortunately the band struck up and dancers began to stream back onto the floor, swallowing them up.

'Sharon . . . you look absolutely stunning tonight,' Norton murmured, letting his eyes drift down slowly over her as he released her. His eyes came back to meet hers pleadingly. 'Don't be angry with me . . .'

Sharon heaved a sigh. What was the point? 'I'm not . . .' she said reluctantly.

'Good, let's dance. This group's got a great rhythm, don't you agree?'

They danced and after a few moments, Sharon began to enjoy herself. Despite his irritating manner at times, Norton had an irrepressible good nature and it was hard to remain antagonistic towards him.

When the music stopped Norton led Sharon over to where most of the nursing staff and their partners were congregated. At this table she was welcomed warmly but had to suffer a few teasing jibes about the company she was now keeping, her rise up the social ladder, and quips about married life. It was all very good-natured and no-one said anything malicious. No-one mentioned Naomi. They were all being very tactful.

Janna was there of course, with Peter. She looked very fetching in voluminous pale mauve harem trousers and top, with her blonde hair flowing seductively about her shoulders. It was obvious to Sharon at once that Peter still had eyes for no-one but Janna.

'You look fabulous, Sharon,' Janna said in her usual generous way. 'I bet Bryce was scared to bring you out when he saw you in that!'

'Do you think it's too . . . provocative?' asked Sharon, still worried about what Naomi had said.

Janna rolled her eyes. 'We . . . ell . . . it does kind of advertise your good points, in an understated sort of way.' She grinned wickedly. 'It's seeing us out of uniform for the first time that makes some of their eyes stand out on stalks!' She added slyly, 'I saw Naomi Forrest a few minutes ago . . . she's in your party, isn't she?'

'Yes.'

'I think *she* looks provocative,' declared Janna. 'Her dress doesn't leave anything to the imagination.'

Sharon said, 'You must admit, she's got everything.'

'Except Bryce!' interrupted Janna firmly.

You're wrong, Janna, she's got him too, Sharon wanted to say but did not.

For an hour she sat and chatted to her friends, and danced with whoever asked her. She was anxious to dispel any feeling they might have that she now considered herself a cut above them because she was married to Bryce and so she stayed longer than perhaps she ought to have done.

At length she said to Norton,' 'I think it's time I went back.'

'Allow me . . .' He jumped up, insisting on accompanying her.

The rock group was just starting another bracket of numbers, and Norton whirled her onto the floor, despite her protests.

'Just one more dance,' he insisted, admiring her openly.

Sharon sighed resignedly, and since there was no point in not doing so, threw herself wholeheartedly into dancing. When the music stopped Norton tucked her arm through his and they began to make their way towards the other end of the ballroom.

Suddenly Norton halted. 'Oh-o . . . where are they off to, I wonder.'

Sharon followed the direction of his gaze automatically. In the centre of one side of the ballroom sliding glass doors opened onto an outdoor patio, but Sharon could not see what had caught his attention there.

'What's the matter?' she asked.

'Bryce and Naomi,' he said succinctly, 'have just sneaked out onto the patio.'

Sharon stiffened involuntarily, and knew that he must feel her tension, although she managed to keep her voice nonchalant. 'I didn't see them.'

Norton glanced at her, his eyes narrowed accusingly. 'You don't want to believe it, do you? You're just pretending it isn't happening. But it is and you're going to get very very hurt sometime soon, Sharon, if you don't face up to it. Come on . . . I'll prove it to you!'

Sharon swallowed hard. She didn't want to go. She didn't want to see. Perhaps, as Norton had said, deep down she was pretending to herself that it wasn't happening, even though she knew it was. Almost brutally he dragged her towards one of the open doors. Sharon could not break away from his tight hold on her hand without drawing attention to herself, so reluctantly she followed.

The night air was warm after the air-conditioning inside the ballroom. It was a clear, starry night, with no breeze to stir the row of stately poplars which lined the river bank beyond the edge of the flagstoned terrace. Street lights on the opposite bank of the river were reflected in the water which glimmered between the trees.

'Romantic setting, this,' commented Norton rather drily, as his eyes darted searchingly up and down the patio. There were a few couples strolling outside, but they were not easily discernible in the gloom. The only light on the patio was from small unobtrusive lights almost at ground level along the outer edge, and the light spilling out from the ballroom.

Sharon could not see Bryce or Naomi. She whispered angrily, 'They're not here. You must have been mistaken. I'm going back inside.'

Norton's grip on her hand tightened. 'No . . . look . . .'

He turned her slightly and pointed. Sharon did not want to look but could not help it. Twenty paces away she saw Bryce, his profile caught for a moment in a shaft of light from the ballroom. The woman with him could only be Naomi. They were leaning against a piece of sculpture of which there were several on the patio. As Sharon looked, Naomi's arms suddenly wrapped themselves around Bryce's neck and drew his head down to hers. As their lips met, his arms clasped hers almost violently above the elbows. Sharon turned her head away, hurt shafting through her like a scalpel plunging into unanaesthetised flesh. If there had been any doubt in her mind it was banished now. Norton said nothing, but pulled her trembling form against him and held her close.

Then he cupped her stricken face in his hands and looked deeply into her eyes. 'What's good for the gander . . .' he whispered, with a smile, 'is surely good for his goose.' And before Sharon could stop him, he was kissing her.

Sharon wrenched her mouth from his. 'Are you crazy?' she demanded angrily.

He would not release her. 'Sharon . . . don't be a fool. You've seen them now, with your own eyes. How much more proof do you want?'

Sharon broke away from him and began to walk quickly along the patio. He caught up with her and slipped his arm around her waist. 'Sharon . . . don't get mad at me. I'm the one who cares about you.'

She lowered the clenched fist she had jammed tight against her mouth and looked at him despairingly. 'I wish I hadn't seen them,' she said with feeling.

Norton sighed. 'You didn't want to be the last one to know, did you?'

It wasn't worth saying that she had known all the time, that what she had just seen had merely confirmed it. In spite of herself she now turned around and looked back down the patio, but the dancing had started again and there seemed to be no-one else outside now except for herself and Norton. Bryce and Naomi had disappeared. Where? Back to the ballroom, or perhaps to stroll by the river where there was more privacy.

She started to walk back to the open doors into the ballroom. Norton followed, his arm around her and she did not shake him off. Not because it was comforting—nothing could be that now—but because she just didn't have the will to rebuff him.

She had only taken a few steps when she realised that someone was standing in one of the doorways looking out. There was no mistaking the tall broad frame silhouetted against the ballroom lights. It was Bryce. He was alone, and looking in the other direction as though for someone. Naomi presumably, although why was not very clear to her.

A sudden madness overcame Sharon in that bleak moment. She turned to Norton and said hoarsely, 'Kiss me again!' She wrapped her arms around his neck, raised her lips to his and saw his startled expression before he co-operated with fervour. Sharon kissed him long and energetically but without intimacy. She just wanted to show Bryce, if he was looking, and she was sure he would be, that carrying on with someone else was not his prerogative.

Breathless, she at last broke away from Norton, and glanced back. She was gratified to see Bryce staring straight at them. The moment she looked in his direction, however, he retreated into the ballroom.

Norton saw Bryce too. He said resignedly, 'I wondered what had come over you! I might have known it wasn't my irresistible charm working at last. You just wanted to teach him a lesson.'

Sharon felt ashamed. It was a shabby thing to have done, a cheap and pointless revenge. What could she possibly hope to gain by it? She clenched her fists in frustration, regretting the impulse that had made her act so stupidly.

She looked at Norton apologetically. 'I'm sorry, that wasn't very fair . . .'

'Forget it.' He dismissed the subject. 'I understand the impulse that made you do it.' He stroked her cheek, smiling. 'Don't let him use you, Sharon. You're too sweet to be used by a boor like that. He doesn't deserve you. They're two of a kind, they deserve each other.'

Sharon did not reply and Norton, without another comment, escorted her back to her party. Sharon made a big effort to appear composed but she was afraid her feelings must show. Bryce and one other couple were at the table, but Naomi and her godfather were not. Presumably they were dancing.

Bryce looked at Sharon with an icy stare as Norton delivered her back, and he did not speak until the young doctor had left again.

Then he asked rather coolly, 'Enjoy yourself?'

'I'm sorry I was so long,' she answered. 'But I didn't like to rush away too soon in case they thought I was just being condescending, joining them for five minutes.'

'I saw you . . . dancing,' Bryce remarked, and Sharon knew by the way he said it, that he meant her to know he had seen her with Norton too. He added dryly, 'You have a lively style.'

Anger almost made her lash out. How dared he censure her when he had been carrying on with Naomi right under her nose! If there had not been other people present she might have blurted out her fury without restraint. Instead, she turned to speak to the woman on the other side of her.

When Naomi and Sir Leslie returned, Naomi gave Sharon an appraising look. 'You're quite flushed,' she remarked. 'It must be all that energetic dancing. You seem to be quite a hit with the young doctors.' She glanced pointedly at Bryce. 'Aren't you jealous, Bryce?'

Bryce said, 'Looks like supper is being served.'

The buffet had been set up in an adjoining room and waitresses were now pushing back the folding doors to reveal tables laden with food. Some people remained standing around the tables in the supper room to eat, others filled their plates and took them back to their tables in the ballroom. Sir Leslie requested that some kind person should fill a plate for him as he felt quite exhausted.

'Of course, darling,' said Naomi, dropping a kiss on his forehead.

Bryce seemed to prefer to mingle with the crowd in the supper room, which surprised Sharon. It was almost as though he was avoiding Naomi. Could it be, she thought, that he regretted the romantic scene with her on the patio. Anyone might have seen them. Bryce was not the sort of man to approve of anyone else flaunting his mistress on an occasion at which his wife was present.

Sharon was certain this was the case when Bryce barely spoke to Naomi for the rest of the evening, and even when they were all saying goodnight, he was almost terse. Sharon, however, caught a meaningful half smile from Naomi as they parted company, and it very clearly said that although she might be going home with Bryce, he was hers after all.

As Bryce swung the Mercedes out of the car-park, Sharon remarked brightly, 'It was a very pleasant evening, wasn't it?'

Bryce turned into the road, changed gears and let several seconds pass before he answered her. At last he said, 'I'm glad you enjoyed it.' He laid slight emphasis, Sharon thought, on the *you*, as though he hadn't. This further confirmed her opinion that he was regretting his indiscretion on the terrace. Even Bryce had a conscience it seemed.

They did not speak again until they were inside the house.

'Would you like some coffee?' Sharon offered.

He shook his head. 'No thanks.'

'I think I'll have some.' Sharon left him and went into the kitchen alone. She did not want coffee either, but neither did she want to prepare for bed with him watching in icy silence. She made a cup of instant coffee and sat morosely at the kitchen table drinking it. When she judged that he ought to be in bed, she went upstairs.

He was not in the bedroom, and through the open door she could see that he was not in the bathroom either. It occurred to her that he had perhaps had the same thought as she had, and was tactfully waiting for her to go to bed first. She shrugged and sighed deeply. What a farce it was!

She kicked off her shoes and unzipped her dress, pausing to look at herself in the mirror. Was the dress provocative? Behind her, the bedroom door opened and she saw Bryce reflected as he came in. He must have gone into his study first, she supposed. Their eyes met in the mirror and Sharon remained as though transfixed, her fingers still gripping the zip although it was completely undone.

And then, his face dark with emotion, almost as though he was in a rage, Bryce strode across the room towards her, grasped her shoulders and spun her round to face him. For one terrified moment she saw the violent naked desire flaming in his eyes, felt his hands roughly ripping the dress from her shoulders, heard its satin folds swish to the carpet. There was no gentleness in the way he tore the rest of her clothes from her trembling body, and then picked her up and flung her down on the bed, falling on top of her, his mouth crushing hers with such passionate fury as she had never before experienced.

A small cry escaped her lips, but suddenly the shock of his assault was totally overwhelmed by a tumult of desire which swept over her like a floodtide, casting out all thought, and leaving her utterly powerless to resist him. Terror turned to ecstasy and she had no will but to respond to him with every fibre of her body.

CHAPTER EIGHT

SHARON woke in the morning still languishing in a haze of love and fulfilment. She turned towards Bryce, but the other side of the bed was empty. Disappointment pricked her lingering euphoria as she stared bereft at the crumpled bedclothes. Neither of them had to be anywhere in a hurry today, so where was he?

She stretched out a hand to touch the still warm place where he had lain, where she had slept so contentedly in his arms, deliriously happy at last. There had been room for nothing in her mind last night but loving Bryce. Everything must have an explanation, she had felt sure, as she was carried along on the tide of his powerful passion, reaching heights of ecstasy she had never dreamed possible.

She lay with her eyes closed, imagining his strong arms still enfolding her, almost embarrassed now by the surge of passion that had consumed them both, and left them utterly spent, astonished at the ferocity with which it had begun, the exquisite tenderness with which it had ended, and refusing to question the whys and wherefores.

Sharon started as the bathroom door slid open, and turned her head. Bryce emerged, a towel around his waist, his dark hair damp and slicked back on top, curling in wet tendrils around his neck. His face glowed from being freshly shaved. She caught a whiff of his sharply astringent, very masculine after-shave lotion, and her longing for him stirred anew. Why had he got up so early?

He approached the bed slowly, and stood for a moment, hands on hips looking at her, his eyes resting on her face. Sharon gazed back lovingly, stirred anew by his broad muscular frame. And his hands, casually placed on his hips as he looked down at her, so skilful with a surgeon's knife, and so skilful too, and tender, in love-making. She was about to lift her arms up free of the sheet, to tempt him down to love her again, as she felt sure he would, when a shadow of something like pain crossed his eyes, making her hesitate.

He said in a flat tone. 'I'm sorry about last night.'

She felt as though she had been steam-rollered. 'Sorry . . .' She thought she had spoken but no sound came out. She sat up, clutching the sheet against her as he turned away to dress. She was utterly perplexed. She had been expecting different words—words of explanation, the end of doubts, words of . . . love. Surely there had been words of love between them last night? Or had she imagined them? Had she imagined last night altogether?

'Bryce . . .' Sharon was so shattered by the unexpectedness of his apology, and his cool manner, that she did not know what to say. 'You don't have to be sorry . . .' she managed to get out at last.

He glanced at her. 'But I am. I shouldn't have lost control. Let's just forget it, shall we? I promise you it won't happen again. In fact I think the time has come for me to move into the spare room. I'll think of some excuse for Betsy.'

'Bryce . . .' It started as a shriek, but finished as a whisper, dying away to nothing as the truth suddenly confronted her.

Like an icy cold shower the realisation almost took her breath away. The ecstasy of the night had turned to nightmare. She was a fool, a stupid fool, to have believed that miracles could happen. Bryce had made love to her for one reason only, because he had been frustrated in his need for Naomi. All night at the ball Naomi had tantalised him. All night their desire for each other had been thwarted, a stolen kiss on the patio their only compensation, and Bryce had felt guilty about that. Seeing his wife half undressed had roused a storm of passion he had been unable to control. He had used her and now he regretted it. He was angry with himself, and with her too.

Sharon slid down into the bed, utterly humiliated, and turned her face into the pillow. Her whole body ached with misery. She heard the bedroom door close as he went out, but still she did not move. She could not even weep.

Presently she dragged herself out of bed and showered, moving like a zombie, steeling herself to be normal and cheerful with Betsy who was eager to hear all about the ball.

Since remaining in the house was likely to increase her despondency, Sharon decided to employ a little therapy, and go for a ride along the river to South Yarra. She would then browse around the antique shops in Prahran until it was time to go on duty mid-afternoon. It might help to take her mind off everything.

'I won't be in for lunch,' she told Betsy. 'I'll grab a snack somewhere.'

'Take care,' said Betsy, who did not approve of Sharon riding her bicycle everywhere. She considered it much too dangerous, and Sharon suspected that she also thought it a little undignified.

Sharon rode to Princes Bridge and crossed to the other side of the river. It was a bright sunny day, a little humid, and there was a bank of cloud low on the horizon in the direction of the bay. Rain later, the forecasters had predicted, but probably not until late afternoon.

Seagulls flew up in front of her, screaming, as she cycled leisurely along the bicycle track near the water's edge. There were few other people about that morning. There was a tramp stretched out on a bench, a newspaper covering his face, and an old lady with a bag of bread feeding the gulls who swooped and squabbled for her largesse. She waved to Sharon and smiled cheerfully. The gulls scattered again, and she called out, 'There's a lot of them here today. We're in for a spot of bad weather, I reckon.'

Sharon waved back and called a greeting. The old woman was probably right. Gulls were supposed to flock inland ahead of bad weather. She hoped it wouldn't rain until she got back.

It was very pleasant riding along beside the Yarra, with the deep green backdrop of the Botanical Gardens on her right, and the roar of traffic muted by the dense canopy of beech and elm and other trees, that everywhere helped the city to breathe on stifling days, and turned hot tarmac roads into cool leafy tunnels.

Sharon had not liked Melbourne at first. After living in a country town it had seemed too big and impersonal, and also terribly dirty. But after her first year as a student she had grown to love the city with its encircling parks and gardens, and its pockets of nineteenth-century architecture amid the ever-growing jungle of stark concrete and glass office towers.

She loved its cosmopolitan atmosphere, the little enclaves where other cultures blossomed and recreated a little of the atmosphere of Europe and Asia. Bryce enjoyed those things too, she recalled with a pang. They had once planned to eat out somewhere different every month until they had run the whole gamut of cooking cultures; Greek, Italian, Chinese, Lebanese, Indian, Indonesian and many others. In some precious moments snatched from busy routines before the wedding they had explored places they both loved and were familiar with, but which they wanted to enjoy together.

Sharon remembered wistfully one Sunday afternoon in St Kilda, drooling over the exotic cakes and pastries in the pastrycooks' shops, and browsing over the outdoor art display. Once they had spent a morning at Victoria Market, going from stall to stall, not buying anything but simply enjoying the hustle and bustle. Determinedly she chased these thoughts from her mind. It only made it hurt all the more.

It was so pleasant in the sun, she eventually stopped and stretched out on the grass in the shade of a peppermint tree, for a while, watching the traffic spinning along the freeway on the other side of the river. Presently she got up and continued on as far as the Chapel Street bridge, where she left the cycle track and rode into the heart of Prahran. The traffic was heavy, with trams and cars flowing in a steady tide along the interminably straight thoroughfare, but this provided little impediment for a cyclist. Sharon loved this district. She and Janna often used to shop at the market and in the dozens of small exotic shops. It was always crowded and busy and for Sharon had an atmosphere she had found nowhere else.

Feeling suddenly peckish, she parked her bicycle against the kerb up a side street near the Jam Factory, and then realised she had forgotten the wheel lock.

'Damn!' she exclaimed. She stood uncertainly beside the bike for a moment, then decided it was probably all right to leave it. She would take a chance anyhow, she decided impulsively.

Since the ugly old red-brick jam factory had been converted into a shopping precinct, it had become something of a tourist attraction, but there did not seem to be many recognisable tourists about today, Sharon observed, as she strolled through the interior courtyards. She did not stop to window gaze in the many attractive little shops, but hurried past the brightly-painted relics of the old jam-making machinery that dominated the courtyards, to a café. Although it was early, the lunch time crowd was beginning to drift in.

'Sharon!'

To her dismay it was Norton who hailed her as she entered the café. He was already seated at a table for two but apparently was not expecting anyone as he beckoned her to join him. She would rather have avoided him today because he was bound to bring up last night and the subject of Naomi, but there was no way to do so without turning her back and running away. So she steeled herself to cope with it. She would have to encounter him at the hospital sooner or later, anyway.

Norton leaned across the table, searching her face intently. 'Well, how's things?'

'Fine,' Sharon lied, averting her gaze and picking up the menu card.

'You look a bit jaded.'

'I had a late night,' she reminded him. 'Didn't we all?'

He continued to look at her steadily, and with pity. 'Sharon . . . you know you can always talk to me. If there's anything you want to talk about . . .'

'Yes,' said Sharon, with false brightness. 'What about cricket? Do you think Victoria will win the Sheffield Shield this year?'

His eyes narrowed and he touched her hand which was absently toying with the salt-cellar. 'You're about as brittle as an octogenarian's hip today. Did you have a flare-up with Bryce?'

Sharon drew her lips tightly together and said crisply, 'There is one subject I do not want to talk about, Norton, not to anyone, if you don't mind. My private life is just that . . . private.'

He was undeterred. 'You can tell me to mind my own business if you like,' he said, 'but your private life is far from private, Sharon. And last night . . .'

'Norton, I don't want to talk about last night,' Sharon snapped.

'Okay,' he agreed cheerfully, 'but any time you change your mind, I'm always willing to lend an ear.'

'That's very thoughtful of you,' Sharon murmured. His persuasiveness almost tempted her to confide in him just for the comfort of talking to someone sympathetic, but she held it back. She would not talk about Bryce to anyone, not Norton, not even Janna. 'Let's talk about something else right now, shall we?' she said with a smile.

Norton complied, and did not mention Bryce or Naomi again. As they were leaving half an hour later, he offered Sharon a lift.

She shook her head. 'I've got my bike. It's just around the corner.'

Norton walked with her to the side street where she had left her bicycle. As she turned the corner and saw it Sharon heaved a sigh of relief. 'It's still there! I forgot the lock and I was half afraid to leave it.'

Norton laughed. Then he said, 'What are you going to do now?'

Sharon glanced at her watch. 'I've got a bit of time to spare. I think I'll just browse in a couple of antique shops. I want to look for something unusual for my mother's birthday.'

'Mind if I browse with you?'

Sharon did not want him to, but she could not be bothered telling him so. She shrugged offhandedly. 'If you like.'

He wheeled her bike and as they passed a cycle store suggested she buy a new lock.

'No, I've got a perfectly good one at home,' she said.

They spent longer in the first antique shop they came to than Sharon had intended. This was because she became fascinated by some cloisonné plates. She decided that one would be a perfect gift for her mother but she could not make up her mind which to choose. Her parents were on holiday in Queensland and would be passing through Melbourne in a couple of weeks on their way home, so she would be able to give it to her mother then.

'She'll berate me for spending so much money!' Sharon said as the assistant was wrapping her purchase.

'I dare say you can afford it now,' remarked Norton dryly.

Sharon glanced at him. Was he envious of Bryce's position and income? It seemed like it. She knew he had wanted to be a surgeon but had not made the grade.

Outside the shop, Sharon said, 'I'd better go home now. Thanks for the lunch, Norton. See you later at the hospital . . . you're on later today aren't you?'

As he was confirming that he would be, Sharon's eyes suddenly became aware that no bicycle was propped against the kerb. 'My bike . . .' she cried. 'It's gone!'

They both stared at the spot where Norton had propped it. They looked up and down the street, in case they had made a mistake or someone had moved it, but there was no sign of a ladies' blue bicycle.

'I was a fool to leave it unlocked,' Sharon wailed. 'Just because I was lucky the first time. I should have bought a new lock when you suggested it.'

'Well, hello there!' A familiar female voice accosted them.

Sharon turned to see Naomi smiling at them in a rather quizzical manner.

'I didn't expect to run into you two down here,' she said, looking from one to the other in a rather speculative way.

Norton said, 'Hello, Dr Forrest. I'm afraid Sharon's bicycle has just been stolen.'

Naomi's eyebrows rose. 'Oh dear, that's too bad. Don't you lock it when you leave it unattended?' Her tone suggested that it was exactly the kind of carelessness she would expect of Sharon.

Sharon who had felt a wave of antagonism on seeing Naomi, as well as being angry with herself for her carelessness, was momentarily bereft of a reply.

Norton said, 'It was okay while we were having lunch at the Jam Factory, and we didn't expect someone to pinch it from right outside the shop. I mean, we could have been looking.'

'Oh, you had lunch together!' Naomi murmured in mild surprise, making it sound like wickedness.

Norton did not rush to explain that they had met purely by chance, and Sharon resisted the urge to do so herself, feeling it would sound contrived. And what did it matter anyway? She was entitled to have lunch with whom she pleased, surely.

Naomi went on, 'Hadn't you better inform the police?

It might turn up. Some kid probably borrowed it and will abandon it somewhere most likely. The police will keep a look out for it.' She laughed silkily. 'Whatever will Bryce say? He will think you're scatterbrained!' She added, 'Why don't you get yourself a car? Riding an old boneshaker is a bit eccentric to say the least.' Her tone showed her distaste.

'It isn't an old boneshaker,' defended Sharon, nettled by Naomi's tone. 'It was fairly new as a matter of fact.' She looked at Naomi levelly. 'And I don't think riding a bicycle is at all eccentric. Bryce likes to ride too.'

Naomi looked surprised. 'I thought he'd given it up years ago.' Obviously she did not believe Sharon.

Sharon said, 'Well, we went for a long ride out from Lilydale once . . .'

Naomi shot her a knowing glance. 'Before you were married, of course! Dear Bryce. I suppose he was humouring you.'

Sharon shuddered involuntarily. It was quite possible that Naomi was right.

Naomi said, 'I could run you down to the police station now if you like.' Her look encompassed both of them.

'There's no need,' Norton said at once. 'My car is just around the corner. I'll take Sharon.'

Naomi smiled winningly. 'Of course. Sharon would prefer that.' She glanced at her watch. 'And I am in a bit of a hurry as it happens. I have a hair appointment shortly.' She smiled sweetly at Sharon. 'I do hope you get your bike back.'

She walked away, very smart in her ice-blue linen suit, her high heels clattering on the pavement.

Norton said scathingly, 'She is the most insincere woman I have ever met.'

Sharon could not answer. She felt very close to tears. It was all too much—last night, having her bicycle stolen, running into Naomi with her barbed comments. Resolutely she swallowed the painful lump in her throat and said wearily, 'I've got a feeling it isn't my day today.'

Norton caught hold of her arm. 'Cheer up! Worse things happen at sea. We'll go straight to the police station and report the theft and then I'll run you home.'

'Have we got time?' Sharon asked anxiously.

'Yes, plenty. You don't take all day to get ready do you?'

He guided her purposefully towards his car and drove to the police station. Reporting the theft did not take very long.

'Full of good cheer and optimism they were, I don't think,' Norton remarked as they left the station. 'How many thousand bicycles a year did he say were stolen? And what percentage recovered?'

'I can't remember now,' said Sharon, 'but they obviously thought we were wasting their time.' She shrugged. 'It can't be helped.'

When Norton's car screeched to a halt outside the house, Betsy was in the tiny front garden weeding. She looked over the wall in surprise as Sharon and Norton both got out. Sharon, who had not noticed Betsy, said to Norton, 'Thanks for everything, Norton. I'd ask you in for a cup of tea but we'd both be late now.'

He patted her shoulder. 'That's all right, sweetheart. See you around teatime maybe?' To her annoyance he bent his head and kissed her. 'Take care . . .'

He drove off and Sharon opened the front gate to find Betsy looking at her rather disapprovingly.

'Who was that young man?' she inquired. 'And where is your bicycle?'

Sharon explained. Betsy said nothing about the stolen bicycle, but she remarked, 'You know it wouldn't have been thought quite right in my day, gallivanting off having lunch with other men when you were married. But things seem to be different now.'

A distant roll of thunder disturbed the stillness of the afternoon, and Sharon realised that it was beginning to cloud over. She said rather tersely, 'I don't gallivant off

having lunch with other men. I met Norton by accident.'
She could tell that Betsy did not believe her, but the
housekeeper said no more and went back to her weeding.

Sharon raced inside and a short while later left for the
hospital without encountering Betsy again. For most of
her shift she was too busy to spare a thought for her own
predicament. There had been two new admissions that
day. One was a nine-year-old Vietnamese girl who was to
have a hole-in-the-heart operation, and who was very
frightened.

Sharon spent as long as she could spare soothing and
reassuring the child, as well as her almost as panic-
stricken parents who were still in the hospital. They were
a young couple who had escaped from war-ravaged
Vietnam several years ago in a rickety boat along with
others, knowing their baby daughter was ill, but not until
recently exactly what was wrong with her. After all their
trials and tribulations, an operation with every chance of
success might almost have seemed a trivial matter, but to
them it was the most horrifying of their experiences yet.

Communication was difficult because of their limited
English, but Sharon persevered, thinking to herself all
the time as they told her their story that the disasters life
had thrown up for this family made her problems pale by
comparison.

Bryce came into the ward while she was talking to the
family, and after a brief acknowledgement of her, a nod
and a cold glance, he more or less took over. The child
was to be operated on by him. Sharon could not help
admiring the way he dealt with both the parents and the
child. Where she had achieved an uneasy acceptance of
what was to happen, in moments he had the child
smiling, all traces of tears swept away. Because he had
once worked in a hospital in Vietnam he knew a little of
the language which helped enormously. In an unhurried
way he spoke to the parents, his authority and confidence communicating itself to them at once. Within a

few minutes they were shaking his hand warmly and eager to put their trust in him. How could she help loving him, Sharon thought.

There was no opportunity then to tell Bryce about the stolen bicycle. Sharon guessed he would regard it as a trivial matter anyway. Besides, there were much more important things she had to say to him, and all day her resolve had been hardening. She had been a coward for too long. The longer she tolerated the impossible situation the harder it would be to extricate herself. Tonight he would move to another bedroom, and it was that which had decided Sharon. Tonight she would have it out with him.

'It's either me or Naomi,' she said fiercely to herself as she watched him walking out of the ward, his back towards her. 'He can't have both of us.'

Late in the afternoon the storm broke and by the time Sharon went up to the canteen for her tea break it had not abated. There were still frequent flashes of lightning and claps of thunder. It was raining heavily. Sharon wondered, as she pushed open the door to the canteen, if Bryce had gone home yet. And where was Naomi? The thought pierced her mind like a diathermy needle.

'Sharon . . .'

For the second time that day Norton called to her as she was standing tray in hand looking for an empty table because she wanted to be alone. She could not see one and now that he had seen her she had no option but to join him.

After a few preliminary remarks about the weather and the stolen bicycle incident, Norton suddenly said, 'I know this isn't your favourite subject right now, but I think you ought to know that this afternoon I happened to see Bryce and Naomi Forrest climbing into her car. They drove off in a great hurry. Now I wonder where they would be going in the middle of the afternoon.'

Sharon simply closed her eyes and counted to ten. 'I don't want to know, Norton.' She spoke through tight lips. She had seen Bryce early in her shift, about four o'clock. She wanted to ask Norton exactly what time he had seen them, but she couldn't bear to. If he had seen them, he had seen them, probably straight after Bryce had been down to the ward.

'Of course it might have been a perfectly innocent errand,' Norton went on, 'but they both looked pretty pleased with themselves when I saw them a few minutes ago.' He looked at her stricken face with pity. 'Sharon . . .'

'Norton, if you don't shut up, I'll leave,' Sharon hissed at him. 'What pleasure does it give you to torment me?'

'None,' he said flatly, then, 'Sharon, why are you so blind?'

Sharon heaved a sigh. 'Norton, I am not blind. I can see as well as you can. Better! I don't need you to keep rubbing it in that my husband is most likely having an affair with Naomi Forrest who just happens to be his former lover!'

Suddenly she realised she had spoken louder than she had intended. A couple of heads at the next table turned and glanced at them curiously. 'Just leave it, Norton . . . please,' Sharon begged. 'And let me cope with my life my way.'

His knees brushed hers under the table, and she drew hers back instantly, but she was not quick enough to prevent his hand reaching for hers and clasping it tightly. 'Sharon, let's go away together,' he said huskily.

'Go away? Norton, you're mad!' If she hadn't felt so upset, Sharon would have laughed.

'I'm serious, Sharon. I'm not such a bad fellow underneath, you know. Maybe if you bothered to find out . . .'

An involuntary smile flitted across her lips. 'You are an incorrigible flirt, Norton, and I have no intention of jumping out of the frying pan into the fire. At the moment you are getting some perverse pleasure out of taking me under your wing but you're not really serious and you know it. A permanent liaison is not for you, and a casual one is not for me.'

'That's a bit unfair . . .' he protested.

'You don't love me,' said Sharon bluntly.

He drew his lips together, piqued. 'You've never given yourself a chance to find out. You might find Bryce Townshend isn't half the man I am.'

'I don't love you, Norton,' insisted Sharon, 'but in spite of your conceit I like you a lot. I'm grateful to you for your sympathy and for trying to help but I don't think your motives are quite what you pretend to yourself and to me. You're envious of Bryce, aren't you, because he's a surgeon and you're not. And besides that, I was never one of your conquests, so you're jealous because he got what you couldn't. It would give your ego a temporary boost, that's all, if I were to run away with you.'

He looked downcast. 'You do strip a person bare, don't you?'

She hadn't meant to be cruel but he had asked for it. 'Come on, drink your coffee,' she said. 'I've got to get back on duty or the Gargoyle will roast me. Why do I always work the same shifts as she does!'

As they both rose to go an announcement came over the PA system. 'Would Nurse Townshend please report immediately to Casualty . . . Nurse Townshend to Casualty, please . . .'

Sharon looked at Norton, perplexed. 'What can they want with me?'

He shrugged. 'Anyone you know likely to have had an accident?'

It had not immediately occurred to her. 'Bryce!' she gasped, and began to run towards the lifts. He could have had an accident on his way home.

'Take it easy,' Norton said, catching up with her and grasping both her shoulders as they waited for the lift to arrive. 'I saw him just before I came up to the canteen.'

But he could have gone after that, Sharon thought. That would have been half an hour ago at least. Norton was still gripping her shoulders when the lift doors opened, simultaneously with a repeat of the announcement summoning her to Casualty.

Sharon gaped when she saw who was stepping out of the lift. It was Bryce. The rush of relief she felt almost overcame her, and if it hadn't been for Norton's restraining hands she might have rushed into his arms. Norton, seeing Bryce, dropped his hands to his sides. Bryce did not look at the young doctor, only at Sharon.

'Did you hear?'

'Yes . . . I thought . . . I can't think why they want me. I'm just going down.' Somebody must be asking for her, she thought, but who?

Bryce held open the lift doors for her and re-entered himself. Norton followed. Bryce said pointedly to Norton. 'Which floor?'

'Three.'

Bryce pressed the button, and also the ground floor where the Casualty Department was situated. When Norton had left them, Sharon stammered, 'There's no need for you to come . . .'

Bryce did not reply. They reached the ground floor and walked along the corridor to the Casualty Department. In the waiting room the first thing Sharon saw was two policemen. The duty nurse beckoned to her.

'The police want a word with you, Sharon.' Her eyes registered curiosity.

'Police?' queried Bryce. 'What do the police want with you?'

'I have no idea,' said Sharon as they walked over to the two constables.

'I'm Nurse Townshend,' Sharon said, and immediately recognised the young constable she had seen in the police station at Prahran that afternoon. It was odd that they were in Casualty, but she assumed it must be to do with her bike. That was a fresh relief. 'Hello,' she said, 'does this mean you've found my bike?'

'Bike?' Bryce echoed. 'What's all this about?'

'I'll explain later,' Sharon said hurriedly.

The second policeman said, 'As we were on the spot we thought we might as well let you know. We got your bike back, Nurse, but it's a write-off I'm afraid.'

'Oh! What happened to it?' Sharon asked.

'The kid who pinched it was riding without lights and got knocked down about half an hour ago in Malvern Road. He's pretty badly smashed up, unfortunately. The ambulance just brought him in. Another car's gone to get his mother.'

'Oh, no!' exclaimed Sharon, 'How awful! If I hadn't been so careless he wouldn't have . . .'

'He'd have pinched someone else's sooner or later,' broke in the policeman grimly. 'We know him. Always in a spot of bother. Nothing serious yet, but give him time. He was playing truant again today of course, and goodness knows what he was up to tonight.'

'I'm very sorry,' Sharon said. 'How old is he?'

'Twelve.'

Bryce said, 'What happens about the bicycle?'

The policeman shrugged. 'We'll dispose of it for you if you like. It's hardly even worth salvaging for parts. Flattened, it was.'

'Please do that,' said Bryce, without consulting Sharon.

'Perhaps you could pop into the station in the next day or two and clear things up with the duty sergeant,' said the first policeman to Sharon.

His companion added, 'And now if you'll excuse us . . . we're in for a busy night with this heavy rain. There have been flash floods all over the city and suburbs. We had a real cloudburst. Roads are pretty dangerous.' His expression was grim. 'I'm afraid you might be a bit busy in Casualty tonight.'

As he spoke the wailing of an ambulance siren penetrated the hospital walls as an ambulance sped towards the hospital. Through the waiting room window Sharon saw its flashing light and as always flinched inwardly.

Another tragic victim of a road smash no doubt.

When the policeman had gone, Bryce looked down at Sharon, his lips taut, his whole expression impassive. 'Seems you had an eventful day,' he remarked.

She grimaced. 'It was so stupid of me. Oh, that poor kid . . . I must go and see how he is.'

'Perhaps you could just explain briefly what happened,' Bryce suggested. 'I take it you were in Prahran . . .' His tone made Sharon feel she had been caught somewhere she shouldn't have been.

'I went for a ride this morning, along the cycle track from Princes Bridge to Chapel Street, then I had lunch at the Jam Factory, and my bike was all right then—I'd forgotten the wheel lock you see—but it was when I left it outside an antique shop—I was buying a present for Mum—it vanished. It was my own fault . . .' She paused, realising that she had not mentioned Norton. It was strange but she had temporarily forgotten his part in the incident. As Bryce did not like Norton, and it was scarcely necessary to mention him now, she did not.

Bryce was saying anyway, 'We can go home together tonight. I'll leave when you finish.'

There was a heavy pause. He was looking steadily at her, his expression still unreadable as he added, 'The situation is intolerable for both of us, isn't it? We can't ignore it any longer. I think we'd better work something out.'

His eyes held hers, not with apology or even regret, but a blankness that gave away nothing of what he was thinking. Sharon felt as though her heart had divided into several pieces. She looked down at the white-tiled floor. It was as though he must have read her thoughts. Hadn't she decided earlier that tonight she must have it out with him? But, of course, after last night, he must have come to the same decision.

'Yes . . . of course,' she faltered, feeling the tears pricking behind her eyes already, and wondering how she would have the strength to endure the inevitable.

She glanced up at him, 'See you later, then.' She turned and walked through into the casualty ward to see if she could find out the true condition of the boy who had been knocked down riding her bicycle.

She found him about to be wheeled to an operating theatre. Broken leg, broken collarbone, two crushed fingers and concussion, she was told. No serious internal injuries had been diagnosed as yet. Sharon felt a mixture of relief and anxiety. The boy's condition was serious, but without the complication of internal injuries he would make a quick recovery. Oh, the silly idiot, she thought, looking down for a moment at the still white face and tousled brown hair, riding without lights on slippery wet roads. And yet she felt partially responsible despite what the policeman had told her, just because it was her bicycle he had been riding.

Back at last in her own ward Sharon found Sister Garland as testy as she had expected because of her prolonged absence. She was also curious about the summons to Casualty. Sharon explained briefly, and was treated to a look that said Sister was hardly surprised at her carelessness, and the terse comment:

'You do seem to have been rather preoccupied since your marriage, Nurse Townshend. I hope you won't start forgetting things connected with your work.'

Sharon bit her lip. There was nothing she could say. After tonight, she thought, stooping to rescue a teddy bear from the floor beside a bed, as she walked down the ward, I shall probably be leaving South City General anyway.

Later, as Sharon was about to go down to the car-park to meet Bryce, Sister Garland, who was still in her office, called her to the telephone.

'Your husband,' she said briefly.

'Yes, Bryce, I'm just signing off,' Sharon said dully into the receiver.

His voice cut across hers abruptly. 'Sharon . . . I can't come now. There's been a rash of accidents in this freak weather, and I'll have to stay and help out with a couple of emergency ops. Some of the night staff aren't here yet. I don't know how long I'll be, so you'd better get a cab and go on home.'

Sharon felt a rush of relief, as well as disappointment. Delaying what they had to say to each other was only prolonging the agony. But she didn't think Bryce was making an excuse to postpone the discussion. Always on a night like this there was a spate of accidents and the operating theatres had to work flat out to cope with the rush.

'All right,' she said. 'See you when I see you.'

There had been no general request for nurses finishing their shifts to remain, so presumably Casualty and other departments were coping. Sharon was half inclined to wait around for Bryce but since that might mean being there half the night, she resisted the temptation and called a cab. At least, she tried to call a cab. She dialled for five minutes but could not get through.

Sharon pursed her lips as she stood indecisively for a few moments by the telephone. It looked as though she might be waiting around for ages anyway, unless she could pick up a cab at the hospital entrance. Cabs came and went quite often and she might be lucky.

As she reached the main entrance foyer a fresh roll of thunder shook the building, and the rain began falling heavily again, the drops bouncing off the tarmac outside so violently the water appeared to be foaming. The concourse was awash and she could barely see the traffic moving slowly along the road outside the hospital gates, the rain was so heavy.

As she paused, staring bleakly out into the night, someone came up behind her. It was Norton.

'Filthy night,' he commented.

She turned to grimace at him. 'And I haven't even got an umbrella!'

'How are you getting home?'

'I was supposed to be going with Bryce, but he's been

held up with all the accidents coming in. It looks as though I might have to wait for him after all since I can't get a cab by phone and it doesn't look as though I'm going to have much luck picking one up on the concourse.'

'Don't bother,' said Norton. 'I'll drive you.'

'No, really you've done enough for me for one day,' Sharon protested, feeling a little regretful now that she had been so blunt with him earlier. She added, 'That call to Casualty, by the way, was the Prahran police. A kid stole my bike and had an accident on it. The bike's a write-off but the boy's going to be all right, I hope.'

'Nasty . . . but one can't help thinking it served him right.'

'Oh, Norton . . . no . . .'

He squeezed her shoulders. 'You're so forgiving. Come on . . . I'm taking you home.'

They walked through to the staff entrance nearest to where his car was parked and hesitated for a moment or two in the doorway.

'If we run for it we might not get too drenched,' Norton said. 'I think it's easing off a bit.'

Together they ran across the glistening tarmac to the car and flung themselves inside breathlessly.

'Not too bad!' exclaimed Norton. 'What about you?'

'I'm all right. I'll change as soon as I get in,' said Sharon.

For a few minutes the car would not start. Norton cursed as he pressed the starter again and again to no avail.

'Water in the engine, I suppose,' he muttered. 'And I guess I'd have Buckley's chance of getting the RACV right now.' He tried again and eventually the ignition caught and the engine turned over, much to Sharon's relief. She was longing to get home now, where she could be alone and compose herself for the ordeal she would have to face when Bryce came in.

Norton switched on the windscreen wipers and backed out of the parking spot. Sharon took a cloth from the glove box and wiped the steamed-up windows. They joined a slow queue of cars in the road outside the hospital, and Sharon began to think they might be stuck in the traffic jam forever, but after the junction with another main road, it thinned out a bit and they proceeded more normally.

'Have you home and dry in two ticks now,' said Norton, speeding up as they approached an intersection where the lights were just changing to amber.

Astonishingly, all at once there were no cars directly ahead of them. Norton put his foot down hard to get over on the amber light. Some instinct made Sharon glance to her left. She screamed as a car starting forward too soon dazzled her with its headlights, and then hit them broadside on.

The lights of the traffic and street lamps and neon signs spun round in a whirl of colour as Sharon heard the deafening sound of tearing metal. She felt nothing, only the shuddering jolt of impact, and then knew nothing more.

CHAPTER NINE

SHARON was vaguely aware of voices. They were familiar voices, but she was too muzzy to put names to them. They came and went, distorted like voices on a bad telephone connection. Even the words meant nothing to her at first, they were just words she seemed to have forgotten the meaning of. But gradually her brain began to focus.

'No, she isn't going to die, Janna.' It was a man's voice speaking, deep, calm, reassuring and very familiar. He went on gently, 'It was touch and go, but she'll pull through.'

'Oh, Bryce . . .' A girl sounding tearful.

Bryce . . . Janna . . . Sharon's drugged brain juggled with the names. Bryce was her husband. Janna . . . Janna was her friend and former flatmate. What on earth were they talking about? Who wasn't going to die? What did they mean, touch and go but she'll pull through? Who were they talking about?

'Would Nurse Townshend please go immediately to Casualty . . .'

Casualty . . .

Fragments of recollection began to stop whirling and stick together. Policemen . . . bicycle . . . a boy who had an accident on a bicycle which he had stolen . . . her bicycle . . . All at once it came back in a rush. The rain, Bryce being delayed, Norton driving her home, and the other car hurtling towards them, headlights blinding her . . .

They were talking about *her*, she realised suddenly. It was she who wasn't going to die, but it had been touch and go. Her eyes flicked open briefly, saw the white walls, the intravenous drip, the screens, the monitors.

Oh, no, she thought, I'm in hospital . . . I must have had an accident.

'Bryce . . .' His name was wrenched from her lips in an unintelligible whisper.

A large hand covered hers. It was warm, comforting. 'Sharon . . .' Then he was saying to someone else. 'She's coming round, Sister.'

Sharon did regain consciousness for a few moments, saw Bryce's face swimming before her eyes, and then remembered that Norton had been driving the car when the accident happened.

'Norton . . .' she whispered, louder now.

'He's all right,' Bryce said in a low voice. 'He was lucky. Hardly scratched.' A pause, and then, 'You were lucky too, Sharon. You're going to be all right.'

She sighed deeply, exhausted, and drifted off into sleep.

For the next few days Sharon alternated between long periods of unconsciousness and brief periods of lucidity. She was dimly aware of people moving about around her bed, doing things to her and the equipment that surrounded her. She heard in a dazed kind of way snatches of conversation, words like 'concussion' and 'post operative shock' and once she was aware of someone holding her hand again. She opened her eyes, expecting to see Bryce, and saw Norton instead.

He was smiling but his eyes were deeply apologetic and anxious. 'Sharon . . . darling . . .'

'Hello, Norton,' she whispered, and managed a faint smile. 'I'm in a bit of a mess.'

'You're going to be all right,' he soothed softly.

They always tell patients that, Sharon thought. You don't say, tomorrow you're going to die. *No, she isn't going to die.* Bryce's words to Janna drifted back. Were they true, or had he just been kidding her friend?

Another time Janna was there, her arms full of flowers, and she was smiling, but her eyes were as anxious as Norton's had been.

'Cost me the earth, these did,' she said, putting the flowers down on the bed where Sharon could see them. She laughed nervously. 'I hope they'll last you a long time!'

'Hello, Janna,' murmured Sharon weakly.

Janna leaned towards her. 'Well, now you're getting a good look at what it's like from the other side of the sheets. Not much fun, is it?'

Sharon tried to smile.

One morning she opened her eyes and saw her mother. 'Hello, Mum,' she said, surprised.

'Hello, darling. Dad's here too.'

Sharon focussed on the other figure and tears filled her eyes.

'I'm sorry,' she murmured.

'Sorry? Dear me, Sharon, you've nothing to be sorry for.'

Sharon said desperately, 'Dad . . . am I going to die?'

He shook his head. 'No, love.'

He looked her straight in the eye and she believed him. Her father never told a lie. Not even to a dying patient if they asked him point blank. She knew that. A slow feeling of relief trickled through her.

'We flew back as soon as we heard,' said Mrs Derwent.

Sharon was momentarily puzzled. Then she remembered. They had been on holiday in Queensland.

'I'm sorry I spoilt your holiday,' she murmured, and gripped their hands tightly in hers.

'Don't you worry about that,' said her father at once.

'Where are you staying?' Sharon wanted to know.

'With Bryce,' said her mother. 'He's been wonderful.'

Sharon lay thinking about Bryce after they had gone. Her mind was still hazy about what had happened but now she remembered that they had been going to talk things over that night, work something out—wasn't that what Bryce had said? Her accident had put paid to that.

The next time he came to see her, she said, 'Bryce, we were going to talk . . .'

He hushed her gently but firmly. 'Not now, Sharon. You just concentrate on getting well. There's plenty of time.'

She was too weary to insist, and later, when she began to feel better, she couldn't bring herself to mention the subject again. Just thinking about it brought tears to her eyes. She didn't feel strong enough yet to cope with emotional problems.

Eventually she learned from Norton exactly what had happened. The car hit them broadside on, spinning them round. He had lost control as the steering failed and the car had crashed into a lamp standard on the other side of the intersection. It was Bryce who told her that her injuries were multiple—severe concussion, several vertebrae damaged, fractured fibula, and as if that wasn't enough, a ruptured spleen, not to mention extensive abrasions and bruises.

'You ought to be dead,' Bryce told her bluntly. 'You sustained the full impact of the car hitting you, and it was the passenger side that hit the lamp pole. That Norton escaped almost unhurt is just one of those extraordinary pieces of good luck that sometimes happen.'

Sharon saw by his face that he didn't think it was fair. But she felt no bitterness herself. It wasn't Norton's fault. She remembered suddenly that he had fastened his seat belt, but she hadn't, for once, bothered.

'I'm not paraplegic, am I?' she demanded in horror as the possibility struck her.

'You can wiggle your toes, can't you?' Bryce answered with a smile.

'Yes . . .' Her panic subsided. She could have answered that question herself if she'd been thinking straight.

'You might have to wear a back brace for a while,' Bryce told her, as he bent forward to smooth a stray strand of hair off her forehead, 'but I don't expect you to sustain any lasting trouble.' He smiled wryly at her. 'No need for me to tell you that you're getting the very best medical care and nursing, is there?'

She shook her head. She knew only too well the dedication of the nurses looking after her, but it was reassuring to have Bryce remind her of it.

One day two strangers came into Sharon's room at visiting time. Sharon looked from one to the other, puzzled. The boy was on crutches, his leg in plaster, the woman who seemed to be his mother was quite young and looked very nervous. They were complete strangers to Sharon and she wondered if they had made a mistake until the woman said, hesitantly:

'Hello, Mrs Townshend. I'm Tania Roberts and this is Brian, my son. He . . . he wanted to come and apologise to you.'

Sharon was intrigued. 'Apologise?' she queried.

'Go on, Brian,' urged his mother.

The boy swung himself nearer to the bed. His face went scarlet but his embarrassment did not quite extinguish the impish look in his eyes, the rebellious lift to his mouth. Sharon had a faint memory of such a face, still and white, framed by tousled brown hair . . .

'I'm sorry, Mrs Townshend,' he blurted out gruffly. 'About your bike . . .'

She knew even before he had finished speaking. 'Oh, you're the boy who stole my bicycle,' she said. The boy's colour deepened and he began to look apprehensive, no doubt expecting her to be angry.

'It was a pretty stupid thing to do,' he rushed on, 'and Mum reckons I got punished . . .'

'The police said your bicycle was a write-off,' said Mrs Roberts, 'but they promised not to lay charges against Brian if he behaves himself and pays you back for it.' She held out an envelope. 'I wrote you a cheque. I . . . I hope it will be enough . . . and I'm taking it in instalments out of Brian's pocket-money.'

Brian screwed up his face, and Sharon suddenly felt

sorry for him. He didn't look all that bad. She took the envelope and held it in her hand, not opening it.

'The trouble is,' Brian's mother said all at once, 'he doesn't have a father. His father and I are divorced and Phil lives in South Australia . . . with his new wife . . . so he doesn't see him all that often, only when Phil comes to Melbourne on business . . . he's with a plastics company . . .' She stopped. 'I'm sorry . . . I wasn't trying to make excuses for what Brian did.'

Sharon had felt a great rush of sympathy for them as Tania Roberts was speaking. She understood what it felt like when your husband abandoned you for another woman.

'I don't think Brian will do it again,' said Sharon with a conviction she really did feel. She frowned at the boy and said with deliberate severity, 'At least I hope not.' The child writhed uncomfortably but said nothing. Sharon fingered the envelope. She wanted to give it back to them but she wasn't sure if that would be wise. Mrs Roberts looked as though she probably couldn't afford the cost of a new bicycle. She wished she knew what would be the best thing to do.

'I'm sure he won't,' said Tania Roberts. 'Sergeant Hicks gave him a pretty good dressing down.'

Sharon suddenly had a brainwave. 'Mrs Roberts,' she said, 'I don't want to take your money, but I think it's a good idea to make Brian learn to be responsible for his actions. I'd like you to take this back, but I'd like the instalments you're deducting from Brian's pocket-money to go to the youth club the police organise.' She remembered seeing a poster for the youth club on the wall at the police station. She looked at Mrs Roberts and her son hopefully. 'Would you think that was fair?'

Mrs Roberts looked taken aback. 'But, Mrs Townshend, it was your bicycle, and you're entitled to some recompense.'

Sharon shook her head. 'I don't want any, but I'd like to see Brian joining the youth club and finding better things to do than stealing bicycles.' She handed back the envelope.

Mrs Roberts still did not take it.

'Please take it back,' insisted Sharon.

Mrs Roberts shook her head. 'No, I can't . . . it wouldn't be right.'

At that moment Bryce came into Sharon's room. He hesitated when he saw that she had visitors but Sharon said, 'Don't go, Bryce . . . you can resolve this little difficulty for us.' She explained what Mrs Roberts had done, and what she wanted them to do. 'What do you think?' she finished.

Bryce smiled at everybody, then, with a twinkle in his eyes, said, 'It sounds typical of my wife, Mrs Roberts, and in any case I always agree with her!'

Mrs Roberts smiled. Hesitantly she took the envelope and put it back in her handbag. 'I really think it's too generous of you, Mrs Townshend.'

Bryce said, 'I'll be back later, Sharon. Goodbye, Mrs Roberts. I hope you're behaving yourself, young Brian. What's this? Who's been scribbling all over your plaster?'

'They're autographs,' said Brian. 'All the kids wanted to sign it.'

'At school? Going to school again are you? Not playing truant?' Bryce fixed the boy with a fierce look.

Brian flinched. 'Yeah . . .'

'Good. You'll never get to be a famous surgeon if you don't go to school.' He paused, his grim look changed to a smile again as he unclipped a pen from his pocket. 'I suppose you'll let me autograph it for you too!'

When he had made a couple more friendly remarks, he left them, and Mrs Roberts, her eyes shining with admiration, said, 'You're so lucky having such a lovely husband! I think he's gorgeous.'

Sharon smiled but her heart ached. Bryce was making a good show of everything being normal. If Mrs Roberts only knew the truth!

The woman went on. 'Brian got to know him quite well when he was in hospital. He idolises him. I don't know if he'll ever be clever enough to become a surgeon, but that's what he wants to be at the moment.' Brian was carefully studying the distinguished signature on his plaster cast.

Five minutes later they left, and Sharon heaved a sigh, not of relief, but of contentment. She felt that she had done the right thing. She wondered if Bryce had really thought so. He did not come back later and in spite of everything she was disappointed.

The only person who never came to see her during the long weeks she was in hospital was Naomi. Not that Sharon expected her to, or minded that she didn't.

At last the day came when Bryce said that she would be able to leave hospital very soon. He held her hand and looked very seriously at her.

'We're keeping you here until the end of the month, and then I think the best plan would be for you to go home to Winnabri to convalesce. Your parents are very keen for you to go, and I think it would do you good to get right away for a while.'

Sharon swallowed hard. It would be marvellous to go home of course, but she knew why Bryce was so keen on the idea. It was virtually an official separation. He had been wonderful to her since the accident, but she knew this must be partly because he felt guilty.

He said, 'Betsy would love to look after you but I'm afraid it might be a bit much for her, and besides I think you'd rather be with your parents, wouldn't you?'

She wanted to say, *I'd rather be with you*, but he wouldn't want to hear that. She really had no choice. She said, almost inaudibly, 'We still haven't talked . . . about us.'

His mouth tightened and his eyes narrowed slightly. 'No. But we will, when you're quite well again. You're in no state to discuss emotional problems now.' He patted her hand. 'In any case I absolutely forbid it.'

The silence that followed, with Bryce looking steadily at her, was so disconcerting, that she blurted out the first thing she could think of. 'How is your research coming along?'

He looked surprised at her interest, and answered, 'Very well. We think we may have stumbled on what you might call the missing link at last. There's no doubt about it, combining experience and ideas does pay off.' A look that was almost schoolboy excitement came into his face. 'This is highly confidential, Sharon, but I think we're going to be able to put our theories to the test very soon. It is really only a matter now of waiting for the right patient, the right circumstances.'

'You deserve success,' she said. 'You've worked so hard.'

'So have the others,' he said at once. 'Naomi is a workaholic, and Chris is nearly as bad. We've gone ahead by leaps and bounds since they joined the team.'

'I'm glad,' murmured Sharon, and was glad when he changed the subject. She didn't want to hear any more how marvellous Naomi was.

The day before Sharon was discharged from hospital, Norton came to see her. He had been one of her most regular visitors, after Bryce, and still felt deeply responsible for her accident.

'I hear you're going home for a while,' he said, 'to Winnabri.'

Sharon nodded. 'Mum and Dad want me to and Bryce thinks it's a good idea.'

'The beginning of the end,' he said tentatively.

She shrugged. 'You know that's a subject I don't want to talk about, Norton.'

'Sorry, but . . .'

'But what?' she queried wearily.

'Never mind. I guess I was just too late. I should have asked you to marry me a long time ago instead of just fooling around.' His face was serious. 'Sharon . . . is it too late? Couldn't we make a life together?'

'Norton, please . . .' she begged. 'It's painful to me . . .'

He took a deep breath. 'I never wanted to marry anyone before.'

'And you don't want to marry me. You just feel responsible for me now because of the accident. It's very noble of you but it wouldn't work. A successful marriage must have love.'

He smiled at her, the confidence not quite gone from his eyes. 'Maybe you'll change your mind when you're brooding all alone at Winnabri.' He lifted her hand to his lips. 'You know where to find me, Sharon.'

Sharon drew her hand away. She hoped she was right and that Norton's hurt was only skin-deep. She knew that she would never feel differently about him.

Bryce came to see her just before her parents arrived next morning to take her home. They had stayed the night at Bryce's house. Sharon, sitting in a chair in her room waiting for them, found that she was trembling when Bryce walked in.

'Well . . .' he said, smiling. 'How do you feel?'

'I . . . I feel fine.' She tried to look as though she really did. Her leg was still in plaster but otherwise she felt reasonably well physically.

'Let me look at you . . .' He raised her onto her feet and gripped her upper arms, looking steadily into her eyes. 'Now, you'll take it easy, won't you, and do what your father advises.'

'Of course.' She felt so weak, looking at him, wanting him to hold her close, yet all the time burning with jealousy. Naomi was there between them as she had always been. No doubt she was pleased that Sharon's accident had finally forced a separation. Sharon wondered if she would ever see Bryce again.

Suddenly, to her astonishment, he drew her against him, held her head against his chest and stroked her hair. 'Poor Sharon,' he murmured, 'it's been a terrible ordeal for you, but the worst is over, and time is a great healer of all ills. Being at home with your parents will give you a chance not only to get really strong again, but to look at things in their proper perspective . . . I hope . . . before you decide what you want to do.'

Tears prevented her from speaking, and sheer physical weakness from being angry with him. He expected *her* to get things into perspective! She must decide what *she* wanted to do! Did he mean that she could remain as his wife, in name only, if she wished? She wanted to ask him to be more explicit but she couldn't find the words, or the composure to say them.

She pulled away from him and reaching for her crutches hobbled to the bedside table, pulling out the drawers although she had already done it, and mumbling, 'Just checking I haven't forgotten anything. Mum and Dad will be here in a minute.'

She was relieved when they arrived. They both hugged her and said how much better she was looking. Mrs Derwent said to Bryce:

'I hope you'll be able to come up and see us, Bryce. You'll miss each other terribly, I'm sure. I wonder if we ought to be taking Sharon away from you but . . .'

'Bryce is very busy with his research at the moment,' Sharon put in. 'He wouldn't have much time to spend with me.' She looked straight at him. 'I won't mind if you're too busy to come up.' There was no gratitude in his eyes for her let-out.

He kissed her dutifully as he tucked her into the back of her father's car, and she could not help thinking how perfectly he had played the role of loving husband during her illness. Her parents had never suspected there was anything wrong, and even Betsy who had visited her frequently had been fooled, telling Sharon how devotedly Bryce had sat by her bedside when she was unconscious. Had any of them been present when she and Bryce were alone together they would have noticed the constraint, however.

Sharon wanted to tell her parents, but it was some time before she summoned the courage to admit to them that her marriage to Bryce was a failure, and why. Even then it was not a conscious decision, but precipitated by events.

Sharon was happy to be back home, and her spirits lightened somewhat despite the heaviness of her heart. It was inevitable, however, that her mother soon noticed that not only did Bryce not telephone, but that there were no letters either. At first Sharon tried to prevaricate.

'I told you he was busy and mightn't have time,' she said evasively.

Her mother looked at her oddly. 'But you haven't phoned him. Aren't you a bit worried?'

Sharon did not know what to say. She realised how foolish she was being trying to hide it now. Bryce had probably assumed she would tell her parents everything. There was no alternative but to do so now, so she reluctantly explained the situation.

Mrs Derwent, naturally, was deeply shocked. When Sharon had finished, she said, 'Oh, my dear, I never guessed . . . what you must have been through. And to say it's been going on ever since you were married. I can't believe it. He seems such a nice man, and so devoted all through your illness . . . so fond of you . . .'

Sharon sighed. 'One has to keep up appearances sometimes.'

'It's too dreadful,' said her mother. 'Your father will be shocked too.' She held Sharon's hand sympathetically. 'My poor darling, and you never said a word.'

'I don't believe in talking about private problems,' said Sharon. 'You have to work them out yourself in the end. Besides, I didn't want to worry you. Bryce and I were going to talk it over the night of the accident. Now he says he won't discuss it until I've fully recovered. My coming here is a start . . . it means we've separated. It will make the rest easier. I expect he'll get in touch eventually.'

'But you say she won't marry him?' said her mother.

'That was what she said before. She might have changed her mind.'

'I really don't know what to say, my dear,' said Mrs Derwent. 'I can only say how sorry I am . . . and then for you to have that dreadful accident on top of it all.'

'Don't be too sympathetic, Mum,' said Sharon bravely, 'or I might dissolve into tears. It has to be faced up to, that's all. I might get in touch with Bryce myself as soon as I feel up to it, if he doesn't contact me.'

There was a subdued atmosphere in the house for a few days after Sharon's confession and she knew her parents were deeply disturbed, and concerned for her. They were also very angry with Bryce, and despite her protestations that it wasn't his fault that he loved Naomi, they naturally hardened towards him.

As her strength returned Sharon soon grew tired of sitting in the garden reading, visiting friends and pretending all was well when it wasn't. Eventually, once the plaster was removed from her leg, she began helping her father in his surgery when he needed extra assistance. For a while she still needed a stick when walking, but eventually she discarded it. By that time she felt she could say she was fully recovered.

There had been no word from Bryce. Sharon believed that he was waiting for her to contact him. She dreaded the thought of it and kept putting off the moment which she knew she must face up to soon. There was no point in letting it drag on forever.

She did have word from Norton, however, with surprising news. He wrote a short letter, very impersonal, just to tell her that he was going to England, probably for a couple of years or longer. He hoped she was improving and wished her well. Sharon wrote back wishing him luck and hoping he would enjoy working in England. It was the last, she felt sure, that she would ever hear from Norton.

One morning she was walking past the small used-car saleyard next to the garage in Winnabri, when she was struck with an idea which rapidly took root and flourished. She had enjoyed being at home with her parents but all at once she wanted to be completely alone. She decided to buy a second-hand car and have a holiday, just driving around by herself, stopping when and where she felt like it. She would go up along the Murray, she thought.

Elated with the idea, she broached it at dinner that night.

Her mother was less enthusiastic. 'Sharon . . . do you really think you should?' Clearly she was thinking of the accident.

Sharon dismissed her anxiety. 'I'm not afraid of driving, Mum, or of having an accident. In fact I've been thinking I might not go back to nursing in the city. I might get a bush nursing position, and I'd need a car for that.'

Her father was also doubtful but he did not try to dissuade her. 'Maybe you do need some time completely alone, away from us too,' he said understandingly. 'It always helps the perspective to view things from a distance.'

Perspective. That was what Bryce had said. But she wasn't going to see things from his point of view, Sharon thought, not if what he wanted was what she suspected. However much she loved him, she could not be a shadow wife.

The next day she persuaded her father to go along with her to look at the car she fancied buying, since his mechanical knowledge was infinitely superior to hers. They chose in the end not the one she had seen on the previous day but a nippy little yellow hatchback that had just come in. Dr Derwent said the model had been proved reliable on country roads and would suit her very well if she took up bush nursing. Sharon was delighted with her purchase and decided to start her holiday immediately. She would be away a week, she told her parents, and traced out with them on a map roughly the route she intended to take, following the Murray River most of the way.

On the morning she was to leave, Sharon was up first for once. She went out to stow one or two items in the car, and at the same time brought in the morning paper which was lying on the front lawn where it was always tossed by the paperboy. Her father usually claimed it first, but as he was not yet up, Sharon glanced through it, mainly just reading headlines.

On the second or third page her eye suddenly rivetted on a headline and a large photograph. It made her gasp aloud. 'New heart-transplant breakthrough?' screamed the headline, and beneath it the smiling faces of Bryce, Naomi and Dr Chris Hargreaves leapt out at her, grouped around a stranger, the patient who had received a transplanted heart.

Sharon stared at it, her eyes blurring, her heart pounding. She could not bear to read the article. It hurt so much simply seeing the triumphantly smiling faces of Bryce and Naomi, united in their success. She folded the newspaper and left it on the table for her father. It had brought it all back with such painful intensity that she was suddenly overcome with almost uncontrollable trembling.

CHAPTER TEN

As soon as she entered the kitchen and saw her daughter, Sharon's mother knew something was wrong.

'Sharon, are you all right?' she asked, coming quickly towards her.

'Yes, of course,' Sharon replied, and immediately dropped the cup she was setting on a saucer. It smashed on the kitchen floor. Automatically she bent to retrieve the pieces of china.

'Here, let me do it . . . it doesn't matter,' Mrs Derwent said, as Sharon apologised shakily. 'It wasn't a good one.' She reached into the cupboard under the sink for a dustpan and brush, and began sweeping up the fragments of cup. She stood up and looked at Sharon who stood numbly by. 'You don't look well this morning,' Mrs Derwent said. 'Do you think you ought to go, Sharon?'

'I'm all right, Mum,' said Sharon, and promptly burst into tears. She fell against her mother's shoulder and wept uncontrollably, while Mrs Derwent held her tight and soothed her as best she could.

'Don't hold it back,' she said consolingly, 'you've needed a good cry. I don't think you've really let go before, have you? Not since it all began.'

Sharon nodded miserably.

'It was bound to happen,' said her mother.

'It was seeing the photograph,' whispered Sharon, pointing to the newspaper on the table.

'Photograph? What photograph?' demanded her mother.

'In the paper. It was a bit of a shock. Bryce and Naomi . . . and another doctor. They've done their first transplant using a new technique. It's wonderful really, at

178

least it will be if they really have solved all the rejection problems.' For a moment or two her misery was secondary to the brilliance of the achievement. It was what Bryce had been working on for years and finally it had come to fruition. If only it hadn't needed Naomi . . . But in spite of her misery, Sharon felt very proud of him.

Mrs Derwent was already looking eagerly for the article. She was absorbed in reading it when Dr Derwent came in.

'Well, Sharon, all set to go, are you?' he asked breezily, then gave his daughter a second look. 'Nothing wrong is there?'

Mrs Derwent looked up from the paper before Sharon could answer, and she said, 'Did you read all of this, Sharon?'

Sharon shook her head. 'No, I couldn't, but I can guess what it says.'

'What's all this about?' demanded her father. 'What's in the paper?'

His wife ignored him and thrust the newspaper into Sharon's hands. 'I think you should read it, Sharon. All of it.'

Sharon read. It was as she expected. There was quite a bit about the first patient to receive a transplanted heart using a new technique that it was hoped would permanently prevent rejection, and give new hope for long term success. There was quite a bit about the patient, the backgrounds of the three doctors in the team who had perfected the new technique, and how a lucky chance had brought them together at a crucial point in each one's researches. There was high praise for the co-operation of South City General Hospital and the university involved, and then finally a few words that almost made Sharon drop the newspaper. She read the paragraph twice, unable to believe it.

'And as if medical triumph was not enough,' the reporter had written, 'this brilliant team had to produce a romance as well. Dr Naomi Forrest and Dr Christopher Hargreaves last night announced their engagement and will be married shortly, before leaving for America, where Dr Hargreaves . . .'

Sharon looked up at her mother without reading any more. 'They must have made a mistake,' she said, utterly stunned.

'They wouldn't make that kind of mistake,' insisted her mother. 'Here, let me look.'

Sharon mutely handed over the newspaper, watching slightly perplexed as her mother turned the pages until she was near the back. She seemed to be looking for something. At last she said, 'Here it is. "Sir Leslie Ponting is pleased to announce the engagement of his goddaughter, Naomi Forrest, to Dr Christopher Hargreaves, son of Mr and Mrs C. Hargreaves of Tonbridge, Kent, England . . ."'

Sharon covered her face with her hands and sank into a chair. 'Oh, poor Bryce,' she whispered. 'She let him down after all. She walked out on him once and now she's done it again. Poor Bryce.'

'I hardly think he deserves your pity,' said her mother tersely.

'I'd say it serves him right,' commented her father just as censoriously.

Sharon was touched by their loyalty. She said, 'It isn't his fault he loves her . . . she's beautiful and clever and very sophisticated.'

'Yes, I can see she's beautiful,' commented her mother, looking at the photograph again. 'But she's hard. Ambitious too, I would think.'

'And takes pleasure in breaking up other people's marriages,' said Dr Derwent bluntly.

'She didn't,' said Sharon with a deep sigh. 'Our marriage was doomed from the start. Bryce and I belong to different worlds.'

'Rubbish,' snorted her mother. 'You both seemed to me to have a very good basic understanding, which is what matters.'

'I meant he's a surgeon, a brilliant one, and an innovator. I'm not in his class. I'm just an ordinary nurse.'

Her mother said thoughtfully, 'Maybe now this has happened . . .'

'No,' Sharon said promptly. 'I couldn't go back to him now, even if he wanted me to.'

This was greeted with silence. Sharon knew they would never see her point of view, so she said no more about it. After breakfast she set off as she had planned. The car drove smoothly, and although her thoughts were all centred on Bryce, heightened by what she had read in the newspaper that morning, she felt surprisingly relaxed. The wide open countryside was peaceful and undisturbed, and quietening to the spirit.

She spent the night in a motel on the outskirts of Swan Hill, and to her astonishment slept better than she had for a long time, although at first the fact that the cabin she occupied had a double bed in it was a painfully sharp reminder of Bryce.

The next day Sharon spent in leisurely sight-seeing around the historic town of Swan Hill, and returned to the same motel for the night, intending to set off again early next morning. She did not plan to travel any great distances, but to meander in an unhurried fashion, stopping when she felt inclined. Although she felt quite well again, and her father who had kept her under close observation throughout her convalescence had given her a clean bill of health, Sharon knew it would be foolish to overdo things. The purpose of her solitary trip was to relax both her mind and her body.

After an evening meal in the motel restaurant, she went back to her cabin and as she did not feel as tired as she had the previous night, she switched on the television, hoping to find a good programme to watch until bed time.

For a couple of hours she was diverted by several comedy shows in succession, after which she switched off the set and was about to make herself a cup of coffee when a knock at the door startled her.

'Who is it?' she called out nervously, expecting it to be one of the motel staff, or perhaps someone who had mistaken her cabin for someone else's.

'Is that you, Sharon?' The man's voice carried clearly through the door. 'It's Bryce!'

For a moment Sharon was too stunned to move. Bryce . . . here! It wasn't possible. She must be hallucinating.

'Sharon . . .' he called anxiously.

It was certainly his voice. She opened the door and saw a very solid Bryce Townshend standing outside. She was so taken aback that she involuntarily retreated a step. He came into the cabin and closed the door.

'What are you doing here?' Sharon moved further back into the room, half turning from him because it was more painful to look at him than she would have believed possible. 'How did you know I was here?'

'I've been asking at every motel for you. Your parents said you would probably be stopping over near Swan Hill.'

'My parents told you . . .' She composed herself to look at him.

A wry smile cracked his sombre face. 'Yes. I telephoned this morning to say I was coming up. They told me you'd gone off for a holiday because you wanted to be alone for a while. Your mother was rather anxious for me to follow you. I think she's more worried about you driving off alone like this than she's letting on.'

'I . . . I was going to contact you after I'd had my holiday,' Sharon said.

Bryce did not reply for a moment or two, then at last he said, 'I didn't want to wait. I wanted to talk to you right away . . . to tell you I'd like you to come back.'

Sharon looked fully at him. 'Come back?' she echoed.

'Sharon . . . we could try and begin again . . .'

Suddenly the arrogance of the suggestion overwhelmed all her longings for him. 'You have to be joking, Bryce! Do you think I can just forget . . .?' Tears burned her eyes.

He stared out of the window at the lights of cars flashing past along the highway. 'No, I imagine that it would take time but . . . well, we are married, Sharon, and we did have something . . . didn't we? In time you'll find it hurts less.'

'It will never hurt less,' she whispered bitterly.

He crossed to where she was standing and placed his hands on her shoulders. 'Sharon, believe me it will. I know. I've been through it too . . . alone . . . and eventually you will get him out of your system.'

Sharon stared at him. 'What do you mean, get who out of my system?'

'Norton, of course.' His eyes glowed with compassion. 'I'm sorry it ended as it did, that he hurt you . . .'

'Hurt me? What on earth are you talking about?'

His hands fell from her shoulders and he stepped back, sparks of anger in his grey eyes. 'You're not going to deny you were having an affair with him?'

Sharon was so shattered by this accusation she could not speak.

Bryce seemed to realise he had gone too far. 'All right, perhaps not that, but you were, and I presume you still are in love with him. Isn't that why you're taking this solitary holiday? You're deeply hurt, as well you might be, now he's gone off to England and it's all over between you.'

Sharon was aghast but she managed to keep calm. In as controlled a voice as she could muster, she said, 'I am not in love with Norton. I never was. I don't know what gave you that preposterous idea.'

The doubt lingered in his face as he looked at her with something like contempt. 'Maybe it suits your pride to say that now when he's let you down, but the evidence shows otherwise.'

'What evidence?' she demanded, outraged. 'Pretty flimsy evidence it must be!'

'Flimsy!' He expostulated. 'Do you call refusing to sleep with your husband flimsy evidence?' Anger contorted his face and his grey eyes smouldered. 'What sort of bunny do you think I felt when you turned from me in disgust . . . when I caught you time after time flirting with Norton, holding his hand, his arm around you . . . Naomi told me how she'd seen you together in Prahran, having lunch together, and you'd carefully omitted to mention that he was with you that day. Even Betsy felt she had to tell me he had brought you home and kissed you. You didn't seem to care who knew it. And you were with him the night you had the accident . . . his was the first name you uttered when you were regaining consciousness. He was at your bedside so often, so attentive, and loving . . .' His voice trailed away in disgust.

Sharon had listened to him, utterly appalled. She had never dreamed he would see it like that, that he had even noticed that Norton was paying her attention. She had thought him too preoccupied anyway. She opened her mouth to speak, but he was surging on as though floodgates had been opened.

'You made a right fool of me,' he said, his eyes darkly accusing. 'I should have listened to those who said in the first place that you were just flattered because I was a surgeon and that you were only marrying me because I was a good catch for a staff nurse. I should have known you'd want to have your cake and eat it too! I don't know why I'm here . . . I must be mad asking you to come back. You'd probably do it all again with someone else the minute you had the opportunity!'

Sharon's hand flew up and struck him forcibly across the cheek, effectively checking his flow of words, and making him reel.

'How dare you!' she cried. 'How dare you accuse *me*! What about you? Carrying on with Naomi the minute she came back. You only asked me out in the first place, didn't you, because Sister Montrose said you were frustrated, and then when you knew Naomi was coming back, you married me in a big rush. That was why you didn't tell me about her, because you thought I might guess you were only marrying me to spite her. And then you found out she wanted you after all, so it was all a ghastly mistake. I knew it, Bryce, the whole hospital knew it, and you didn't care that I was being humiliated. That's why I couldn't sleep with you, I didn't want to be a . . . a substitute!'

There was a moment's deathly silence, then he said quietly, 'I haven't been carrying on with Naomi. It's true that one reason for my wanting to marry you in a hurry was so that when she returned she would find me a married man, but I didn't ask you to marry me to spite her. If you must know, the real reason I didn't tell you she was coming back was because I was afraid you would think that! And believe me, Sharon, my biggest reason for wanting to be married straight away was because I wanted you more than I have ever wanted a woman. I was so afraid of losing you.' He added dryly. 'As for what Sister Montrose might have said about me, I haven't the faintest idea.'

Sharon heard but was too wound up to heed his protestations. It was too late. Suddenly it was all pouring out of her too, every detail of the evidence against him, a torrent of words that released the pent-up emotion of months until she reached screaming point.

As she became more shrilly incoherent, he reached out and grasped her shoulders firmly and shook her. 'Stop it, Sharon! You're hysterical. If you don't stop, I shall have to slap your face!'

Sharon wrenched wildly away from him. 'Leave me alone!' She sank onto the bed, her shoulders hunched, wanting to cry, but too tightly wound even to do that.

He sat beside her and wound his arms around her although she turned her back on him. 'Sharon,' he whispered against her shoulder, 'Believe me, you've just said a lot of things that are not true. You've imagined it all.'

'I didn't imagine you kissing Naomi at the ball!' she flared at him.

'And I didn't imagine you kissing Norton, did I?' he countered, while she bit her lip, unable to deny it.

He said quietly after a pause, 'You have denied having an affair with Norton, or even being in love with him. I certainly have not been carrying on, as you put it, with Naomi. So, obviously we both have a lot of explaining to do!'

Sharon turned her head and looked at him. 'I'll say you have! What about Norton seeing you and Naomi going off somewhere together that afternoon . . . the day we had the accident?'

Bryce's eyebrows rose. 'He certainly did not see me. Naomi and Chris perhaps, but not me.'

Sharon had no answer. Was he speaking the truth, and had Norton lied to suit his own ends?

Bryce went on reasonably, 'I wonder if I'm beginning to see the light. Let's go back to the beginning and straighten things out. First let me tell you about Naomi. When I first knew Naomi wanted to come back—she had hinted to Sir Leslie that she would like to, and of course he was quite keen to have her around again—it was a bit of a shock, but there was no good reason for me to refuse to have her in the unit. It wasn't my decision anyway, it was the unit Director's and in view of her work in America which complemented mine, professionally she was very desirable.'

'In other ways too,' Sharon put in dryly.

'Once I would have thought so, but not after I met you. For months, Sharon, I wanted to ask you out, but I couldn't seem to get around to it. There was a barrier I didn't know how to break down. You were always so distant. Then that concert cropped up, but it wasn't an unqualified success. I didn't feel I'd made much of a hit with you that night, and worse, the next day I saw you kissing Norton in the lift. I surprised myself by being jealous, so I resolved to keep away from you, but I couldn't. And in the end, well it seemed you were interested in me after all.'

'Go on about Naomi,' said Sharon.

'Naturally I was always afraid that if she did come back I would still feel something for her, but when it happened there was nothing. Whatever there had been before had been obliterated—by you.'

Sharon did not dare to believe him. He must be deceiving her. But why?

'Naomi is a very forceful personality,' Bryce went on, 'and she likes to be Number One. She was shocked to discover that I was married. Unfortunately, Sir Leslie hadn't told her, which was perhaps unwise of him. She resented my marrying because, although she didn't want me, she didn't want anyone else to have me. She pretended to herself that I still loved her, in spite of you, and I suspect now that she deliberately set out to break up our marriage by insinuating things about you and Norton.

'She hated me for no longer being her slave. That night at the ball she made one last effort to prove her power over me. She said she must talk to me privately and so we went out onto the patio. She said she knew you were having an affair with Norton. She wouldn't say precisely how she knew, only that it was direct from the horse's mouth, which I took to mean that he had admitted it. She was very sympathetic and said that in the circumstances, I needn't feel guilty about wanting her. She kissed me, which you saw, but you couldn't have seen what happened next. She's quite a small person . . .' He smiled at the recollection. 'I grabbed her arms and lifted her up and set her down very firmly two feet away from me and told her not to behave like an idiot, that it was still finished between her and me whatever you did. She was shocked when I stalked off and left her. I felt a bit badly about what I'd done, so at the door I looked around for her, hoping we could be reasonable about it, but she'd gone. It was then that I saw you and Norton . . . kissing very passionately.'

Sharon said quickly. 'It wasn't like that at all.'

'Hadn't you better tell me how it was,' he urged softly.

Sharon hardly knew where to begin. She felt so confused. 'Norton was jealous of you,' she said slowly, and saw Bryce's eyebrows rise in surprise. 'Partly because he had failed to make it as a surgeon, and then because I married you. He wasn't keen on me before that . . . except to flirt with. I had never gone out with him, but when he thought you and Naomi were resuming your old relationship he started paying more attention to me. He was sympathetic, and I like him in a friendly way, but I was never in love with him. That time he kissed me in the lift, was just to let you, or anyone, see him doing it. That night at the ball he saw you and Naomi go outside and dragged me out to witness it. I was so hurt that when I saw you looking, I made him kiss me just to show I didn't care.' She smiled sheepishly. 'I felt so ashamed afterwards. It was a cheap silly thing to have done and Norton knew why I did it.'

Bryce said slowly, 'The night after the wedding when you rejected me, I thought it was just nerves at first, and later I wanted to talk to you about it and reassure you, but when I found you dashing all over the hospital looking for Norton I believed I knew the real cause. I thought you realised you had made a mistake marrying me.'

'I rejected you because of Naomi,' Sharon said soberly. 'I couldn't bear to think of you making love to her . . . or rather making love to me but wanting her. Afterwards I thought maybe I'd been a fool jumping to conclusions so I went up to Cardiology to see you because I couldn't wait to talk to you until we got home. But I saw you and Naomi together and I couldn't say what I'd meant to, so I pretended to be looking for someone. Norton was the only name I could think of on the spur of the moment.

And then after you went to her flat for the evening, and later said "we can't go on like this", I thought you had realised you'd made a ghastly mistake and you wanted to tell me about her.'

'I wanted to talk about you and Norton,' he said in low tones. 'I would have let you go if that was what you really wanted. I thought you'd been out with him that night, not at Janna's.'

They looked at each other for a long moment, then Sharon said, 'Bryce . . . the night of the ball . . . and afterwards . . .'

'I was mad with jealousy after seeing you in Norton's arms. I think I wanted to prove to you that I was a better lover than he'd ever be!' He laughed softly. 'Such pride! Next morning I was ashamed of having forced you into a response you hadn't really wanted to give.'

'But I did want to give . . . When you apologised I thought you'd just used me because you couldn't have Naomi.'

Bryce dragged a hand wearily across his brow. 'And I thought I'd just been a substitute for Norton.' He held her in his arms, lovingly. 'Sharon . . . that night they brought you in . . . I was sure you were going to die. I wanted to die too. I realised then just how much I loved you, and I knew that either way I was going to lose you. I almost wished you would die so Norton couldn't have you. I was glad when your parents wanted to take you home to convalesce. I wanted you out of his way . . . all along I had hoped it might burn itself out and you would get over him, if I gave you time. I threw myself into my work and tried not to think about you. I was absolutely astonished when I heard that Norton was going off to England, and strangely enough I felt sorry for you.'

'I felt sorry for you,' Sharon murmured, 'when I thought Naomi had let you down again.'

He chuckled softly. 'I only hope Chris realises what he's taken on marrying Naomi. He was infatuated with her from the day they first met.'

'Perhaps she'll be different with him,' suggested Sharon.

He shrugged. 'Maybe.'

There was a long silence during which neither of them moved. Each was thinking over what the other had said, finding answers to all the unanswered questions now, in their own minds. Eventually Sharon said:

'I'm sorry, I haven't congratulated you. I saw the article in the paper, and the photograph.'

Bryce shook his head. 'It wasn't just me. It was a team effort. I might still be floundering but for the other two. I'll say one thing for Naomi, she was damned useful!' He laughed.

'It's a wonderful achievement,' said Sharon admiringly.

'Only time will confirm that,' Bryce said cautiously. 'If Tom Grace is still alive in twenty-five years, then I'll rate it a success.'

'Oh, Bryce!' she exclaimed. 'You're much too modest.'

'And so, my darling, are you,' he replied, dropping a kiss on her forehead. 'That's what first attracted me to you . . . that and your very special way with children.' He looked deeply into her eyes. 'Sharon, I wish you knew how much I love you.'

'You never said you did before.'

'Didn't I?' He was genuinely surprised. 'I must have done!'

'I never heard you.' Sharon smiled forgivingly. 'But it doesn't matter, I know now.'

He pulled her head against his chest, stroking her cheek and running his fingers through her hair. 'So that was part of the trouble . . . I'm sorry. I loved you for a long time before I plucked up the courage to ask you out. I was always afraid of committing myself after the disaster of Naomi. I avoided women for years, but you got under my skin. I thought you must have noticed I was in and out of Pinocchio far more than I needed to be!'

'I thought you just liked children.'

'I do, but they weren't the only attraction. In the end, after accidentally discovering you liked Beethoven, I threw caution to the winds and bought tickets to that concert, weeks ahead, but I hesitated to invite you until the last minute in case you said no. I am quite a bit older than you after all, and when I saw you in Norton's arms the day after our date, I nearly didn't ask you out again. I thought you might have just been humouring me. In the end I couldn't help myself.' He laughed softly. 'I decided I would ask you to marry me before Norton had a chance to!'

'I never dared imagine I could love . . . marry . . . someone like you,' Sharon said.

'Why ever not?'

'I'm not like Naomi.'

He smoothed her hair tenderly back from her face. 'Why do you always under-rate yourself? You might not be a brilliant doctor, but you'd make two of Naomi in every other way.'

'Does that mean you're greedy?'

He laughed. 'Yes. Very. For you.' He tilted her face up to his and touched her lips tenderly with his. 'Are you sure you love me?'

'Oh, Bryce, of course I do. So much. I can hardly believe that you love me too.' Sharon smiled wryly. 'I feel so ashamed now, being so jealous, not trusting you.'

'How do you think I feel?' he answered, adding ruefully, 'Sir Leslie Ponting told me that in his opinion you were definitely the faithful kind and I was lucky, but that was the night of the ball, and I couldn't believe him.'

Sharon said, 'Janna always believed in you.'

'Let's forget all that now,' said Bryce, looking fondly at her. 'We're together again and that's all that matters.' His hold on her tightened. 'We've got a lot of lost time to make up.' He bent his head to hers and kissed her long and tenderly with just a hint of burgeoning passion. Sharon responded with joy, her whole body glowing with a sense of well-being such as she had not experienced before. This was not just passion, this was love as well, and this time it was real. After a few moments, Bryce raised his lips and said:

'I can take a couple of weeks off now. Naomi and Chris will keep an eye on our special patient. So, don't you think it's time we had a honeymoon?'

Sharon smiled at him, happily. 'If you say so. Where shall we go?'

Bryce looked around the room and there was a gleam in his eyes as he turned back to Sharon. 'I suppose this would be as good a place as any to stay for a start. This cabin does have the advantage of a double bed!'

They collapsed across it, laughing in each other's arms, as their lips and bodies came together with the promise of real happiness at last.